PRAISE FOR *KN*
FOURTH OF JULY

Lefty Finalist for Best Humorous Mystery

"*Knee High by the Fourth of July* . . . kept me hooked from beginning to end. I enjoyed every page!"

— Sammi Carter, author of the Candy Shop Mysteries

"Sweet, nutty, evocative of the American heartland, and utterly addicting."

— The Strand

"[The] humor transcends both genders and makes for a delightful romp."

— *Fergus Falls Journal*

"Mira . . . is an amusing heroine in a town full of quirky characters."

— *Kirkus Reviews*

"Lourey's rollicking good cozy planted me in the heat of a Minnesota summer for a laugh-out-loud mystery ride."

— Leann Sweeney, bestselling author

PRAISE FOR *JUNE BUG*

"Jess Lourey is a talented, witty, and clever writer."

— Monica Ferris, author of the Needlecraft Mysteries

"Don't miss this one—it's a hoot!"
—William Kent Krueger, *New York Times* bestselling author

"With just the right amount of insouciance, tongue-in-cheek sexiness, and plain common sense, Jess Lourey offers up a funny, well-written, engaging story . . . Readers will thoroughly enjoy the well-paced ride."
—Carl Brookins, author of *The Case of the Greedy Lawyers*

PRAISE FOR *MAY DAY*

"Jess Lourey writes about a small-town assistant librarian, but this is no genteel traditional mystery. Mira James likes guys in a big way, likes booze, and isn't afraid of motorcycles. She flees a dead-end job and a dead-end boyfriend in Minneapolis and ends up in Battle Lake, a little town with plenty of dirty secrets. The first-person narrative in *May Day* is fresh, the characters quirky. Minnesota has many fine crime writers, and Jess Lourey has just entered their ranks!"
—Ellen Hart, award-winning author of the Jane Lawless and Sophie Greenway series

"This trade paperback packed a punch . . . I loved it from the get-go!"
—*Tulsa World*

"What a romp this is! I found myself laughing out loud."
—*Crimespree Magazine*

"Mira digs up a closetful of dirty secrets, including sex parties, cross-dressing, and blackmail, on her way to exposing the killer. Lourey's debut has a likable heroine and surfeit of sass."
—*Kirkus Reviews*

PRAISE FOR *THE TAKEN ONES*

Short-listed for the 2024 Edgar Award for Best Paperback Original

"Setting the standard for top-notch thrillers, *The Taken Ones* is smart, compelling, and filled with utterly real characters. Lourey brings her formidable storytelling talent to the game and, on top of that, wows us with a deft stylistic touch. This is a one-sitting read!"
—Jeffery Deaver, author of *The Bone Collector* and *The Watchmaker's Hand*

"*The Taken Ones* has Jess Lourey's trademark of suspense all the way. A damaged and brave heroine, an equally damaged evildoer, and missing girls from long ago all combine to keep the reader rushing through to the explosive ending."
—Charlaine Harris, *New York Times* bestselling author

"Lourey is at the top of her game with *The Taken Ones*. A master of building tension while maintaining a riveting pace, Lourey is a hell of a writer on all fronts, but her greatest talent may be her characters. Evangeline Reed, an agent with the Minnesota Bureau of Criminal Apprehension, is a woman with a devastating past and the haunting ability to know the darkest crimes happening around her. She is also exactly the kind of character I would happily follow through a dozen books or more. In awe of her bravery, I also identified with her pain and wanted desperately to protect her. Along with an incredible cast of support characters, *The Taken Ones* will break your heart wide open and stay with you long after you've turned the final page. This is a 2023 must read."
—Danielle Girard, *USA Today* and Amazon #1 bestselling author of *Up Close*

PRAISE FOR *THE QUARRY GIRLS*

Winner of the 2023 Anthony Award for Best Paperback Original

Winner of the 2023 Minnesota Book Award for Genre Fiction

"Few authors can blend the genuine fear generated by a sordid tale of true crime with evocative, three-dimensional characters and mesmerizing prose like Jess Lourey. Her fictional stories feel rooted in a world we all know but also fear. *The Quarry Girls* is a story of secrets gone to seed, and Lourey gives readers her best novel yet—which is quite the accomplishment. Calling it: *The Quarry Girls* will be one of the best books of the year."

—Alex Segura, acclaimed author of *Secret Identity*, *Star Wars Poe Dameron: Free Fall*, and *Miami Midnight*

"Jess Lourey once more taps deep into her Midwest roots and childhood fears with *The Quarry Girls*, an absorbing, true crime–informed thriller narrated in the compelling voice of young drummer Heather Cash as she and her bandmates navigate the treacherous and confusing ground between girlhood and womanhood one simmering and deadly summer. Lourey conveys the edgy, hungry restlessness of teen girls with a touch of Megan Abbott while steadily intensifying the claustrophobic atmosphere of a small 1977 Minnesota town where darkness snakes below the surface."

—Loreth Anne White, *Washington Post* and Amazon Charts bestselling author of *The Patient's Secret*

"Jess Lourey is a master of the coming-of-age thriller, and *The Quarry Girls* may be her best yet—as dark, twisty, and full of secrets as the tunnels that lurk beneath Pantown's deceptively idyllic streets."
—Chris Holm, Anthony Award–winning author of *The Killing Kind*

PRAISE FOR *BLOODLINE*

Winner of the 2022 Anthony Award for Best Paperback Original

Winner of the 2022 ITW Thriller Award for Best Paperback Original

Short-listed for the 2021 Goodreads Choice Awards

"Fans of *Rosemary's Baby* will relish this."
—*Publishers Weekly*

"Based on a true story, this is a sinister, suspenseful thriller full of creeping horror."
—*Kirkus Reviews*

"Lourey ratchets up the fear in a novel that verges on horror."
—*Library Journal*

"In *Bloodline*, Jess Lourey blends elements of mystery, suspense, and horror to stunning effect."
—*BOLO Books*

"Inspired by a true story, it's a creepy page-turner that has me eager to read more of Ms. Lourey's works, especially if they're all as incisive as this thought-provoking novel."

—Criminal Element

"*Bloodline* by Jess Lourey is a psychological thriller that grabbed me from the beginning and didn't let go."

—*Mystery & Suspense Magazine*

"*Bloodline* blends page-turning storytelling with clever homages to such horror classics as *Rosemary's Baby*, *The Stepford Wives*, and *Harvest Home*."

—*Toronto Star*

"*Bloodline* is a terrific, creepy thriller, and Jess Lourey clearly knows how to get under your skin."

—Bookreporter

"[A] tightly coiled domestic thriller that slowly but persuasively builds the suspense."

—*South Florida Sun Sentinel*

"I should know better than to pick up a new Jess Lourey book thinking I'll just peek at the first few pages and then get back to the book I was reading. Six hours later, it's three in the morning and I'm racing through the last few chapters, unable to sleep until I know how it all ends. Set in an idyllic small town rooted in family history and horrific secrets, *Bloodline* is *Pleasantville* meets *Rosemary's Baby*. A deeply unsettling, darkly unnerving, and utterly compelling novel, this book chilled me to the core, and I loved every bit of it."

—Jennifer Hillier, author of *Little Secrets* and the award-winning *Jar of Hearts*

"Jess Lourey writes small-town Minnesota like Stephen King writes small-town Maine. *Bloodline* is a tremendous book with a heart and a hacksaw . . . and I loved every second of it."
—Rachel Howzell Hall, author of the critically acclaimed novels *And Now She's Gone* and *They All Fall Down*

PRAISE FOR *UNSPEAKABLE THINGS*

Winner of the 2021 Anthony Award for Best Paperback Original

Short-listed for the 2021 Edgar Awards and 2020 Goodreads Choice Awards

"The suspense never wavers in this page-turner."
—*Publishers Weekly*

"The atmospheric suspense novel is haunting because it's narrated from the point of view of a thirteen-year-old, an age that should be more innocent but often isn't. Even more chilling, it's based on real-life incidents. Lourey may be known for comic capers (*March of Crimes*), but this tense novel combines the best of a coming-of-age story with suspense and an unforgettable young narrator."
—*Library Journal* (starred review)

"Part suspense, part coming-of-age, Jess Lourey's *Unspeakable Things* is a story of creeping dread, about childhood when you know the monster under your bed is real. A novel that clings to you long after the last page."
—Lori Rader-Day, Edgar Award–nominated author of *Under a Dark Sky*

"A noose of a novel that tightens by inches. The squirming tension comes from every direction—including the ones that are supposed to be safe. I felt complicit as I read, as if at any moment I stopped I would be abandoning Cassie, alone, in the dark, straining to listen and fearing to hear."

—Marcus Sakey, bestselling author of *Brilliance*

"*Unspeakable Things* is an absolutely riveting novel about the poisonous secrets buried deep in towns and families. Jess Lourey has created a story that will chill you to the bone and a main character who will break your heart wide open."

—Lou Berney, Edgar Award–winning author of *November Road*

"Inspired by a true story, *Unspeakable Things* crackles with authenticity, humanity, and humor. The novel reminded me of *To Kill a Mockingbird* and *The Marsh King's Daughter*. Highly recommended."

—Mark Sullivan, bestselling author of *Beneath a Scarlet Sky*

"Jess Lourey does a masterful job building tension and dread, but her greatest asset in *Unspeakable Things* is Cassie—an arresting narrator you identify with, root for, and desperately want to protect. This is a book that will stick with you long after you've torn through it."

—Rob Hart, author of *The Warehouse*

"With *Unspeakable Things*, Jess Lourey has managed the near-impossible, crafting a mystery as harrowing as it is tender, as gut-wrenching as it is lyrical. There is real darkness here, a creeping, inescapable dread that more than once had me looking over my own shoulder. But at its heart beats the irrepressible—and irresistible—spirit of its . . . heroine, a young woman so bright and vital and brave she kept even the fiercest monsters at bay. This is a book that will stay with me for a long time."

—Elizabeth Little, *Los Angeles Times* bestselling author of *Dear Daughter* and *Pretty as a Picture*

PRAISE FOR *THE CATALAIN BOOK OF SECRETS*

"Life-affirming, thought-provoking, heartwarming, it's one of those books which—if you happen to read it exactly when you need to—will heal your wounds as you turn the pages."

—Catriona McPherson, Agatha, Anthony, Macavity, and Bruce Alexander Award–winning author

"Prolific mystery writer Lourey tells of a matriarchal clan of witches joining forces against age-old evil . . . The novel is tightly plotted, and Lourey shines when depicting relationships—romantic ones as well as tangled links between Catalains . . . Lourey emphasizes the ties that bind in spite of secrets and resentment."

—*Kirkus Reviews*

"Lourey expertly concocts a Gothic fusion of long-held secrets, melancholy, and resolve . . . Exquisitely written in naturally flowing, expressive language, the book delves into the special relationships between sisters, and mothers and daughters."

—*Publishers Weekly*

PRAISE FOR *SALEM'S CIPHER*

"A fast-paced, sometimes brutal thriller reminiscent of Dan Brown's *The Da Vinci Code*."

—*Booklist* (starred review)

"A hair-raising thrill ride."

—*Library Journal* (starred review)

"The fascinating historical information combined with a storyline ripped from the headlines will hook conspiracy theorists and action addicts alike."

—*Kirkus Reviews*

"Fans of *The Da Vinci Code* are going to love this book . . . One of my favorite reads of 2016."

—*Crimespree Magazine*

"This suspenseful tale has something for absolutely everyone to enjoy."

—*Suspense Magazine*

PRAISE FOR *MERCY'S CHASE*

"An immersive voice, an intriguing story, a wonderful character— highly recommended!"

—Lee Child, #1 *New York Times* bestselling author

"Both a sweeping adventure and race-against-time thriller, *Mercy's Chase* is fascinating, fierce, and brimming with heart—just like its heroine, Salem Wiley."

—Meg Gardiner, author of *Into the Black Nowhere*

"Action-packed, great writing taut with suspense, an appealing main character to root for—who could ask for anything more?"

—Buried Under Books

PRAISE FOR *REWRITE YOUR LIFE: DISCOVER YOUR TRUTH THROUGH THE HEALING POWER OF FICTION*

"Interweaving practical advice with stories and insights garnered in her own writing journey, Jessica Lourey offers a step-by-step guide for writers struggling to create fiction from their life experiences. But this book isn't just about writing. It's also about the power of stories to transform those who write them. I know of no other guide that delivers on its promise with such honesty, simplicity, and beauty."

—William Kent Krueger, *New York Times* bestselling author of the Cork O'Connor series and *Ordinary Grace*

KNEE HIGH
BY THE
FOURTH OF
JULY

OTHER TITLES BY JESS LOUREY

MURDER BY MONTH MYSTERIES

May Day

June Bug

Knee High by the Fourth of July

August Moon

September Mourn

October Fest

November Hunt

December Dread

January Thaw

February Fever

March of Crimes

April Fools

STEINBECK AND REED THRILLERS

The Taken Ones

The Reaping

THRILLERS

The Quarry Girls

Litani

Bloodline

Unspeakable Things

SALEM'S CIPHER THRILLERS

Salem's Cipher

Mercy's Chase

GOTHIC SUSPENSE

The Catalain Book of Secrets

Seven Daughters

CHILDREN'S BOOKS

Leave My Book Alone! Starring Claudette, a Dragon with Control Issues

YOUNG ADULT

A Whisper of Poison

NONFICTION

Rewrite Your Life: Discover Your Truth Through the Healing Power

of Fiction

KNEE HIGH BY THE FOURTH OF JULY

JESS LOUREY

THOMAS & MERCER

Text copyright © 2007, 2018, 2024 by Jess Lourey
All rights reserved.

Published by Thomas & Mercer, Seattle

www.apub.com

Amazon, the Amazon logo, and Thomas & Mercer are trademarks of Amazon.com, Inc., or its affiliates.

ISBN-13: 9781662519277 (paperback)
ISBN-13: 9781662519260 (digital)

Cover design and illustration by Sarah Horgan

Printed in the United States of America

KNEE HIGH
BY THE
FOURTH OF
JULY

Chapter 1

I stepped out of the shower into the sauna of my bathroom, wrapped a towel around my wet hair, and crossed the house to flick on the morning news. The droplets of water on my naked body felt deliciously cool against the already muggy air.

Rinnng.

I jumped. A phone call while the sun was still pinking the horizon never boded well, particularly for someone like me, who was lucky enough to have been within two feet of one fake corpse and two real ones in as many months. I let down my hair and rubbed it, stirring up the spicy smell of rosemary-ginger shampoo.

Ring.

I tossed the towel over the back of a chair and reached for a pair of tattered jean shorts.

Ring.

I threaded the button fly and grabbed a midnight-blue tank top with a built-in shelf bra to rein in the booblets.

Ring.

My answering machine clicked over. Whoever was calling hung up rather than leave a message.

Must not've been important.

I unclenched my shoulder blades and went to brush my teeth. I squeezed out a pea-size glop of Tom's of Maine cinnamon toothpaste, trickled a little water on it, and started scrubbing.

Ring.

Curse words. I ran through a list of people I knew who could be dead or hurt, who I owed money to, or who might be mad at me.

Ring.

The sigh came from the bottom of my soul. I was gonna have to answer that phone. A few years ago, I could have ignored it, but the older I got, the less reliable my denial mechanism became. I wondered what other cruel tricks my looming thirties had in store for me. That simultaneous-wrinkles-and-pimples gag was my favorite so far. "Hello?"

"Mira James, please." The deep voice had an East Coast inflection and a monotone delivery, as if he were reading off a card.

"Speaking."

"Hello, Ms. James!" I could almost see the exclamation point quivering in the air. "How are you today?"

"I'm fine. How are you?"

"I'm good, thank you! Tell me, Ms. James, has love found you?"

I pulled the cordless phone away from my head, studied it, found no hidden cameras, and pressed it back against my ear. "What's this about?"

"It's about helping you find love. Are you single or married?"

"Who *is* this? Are you asking me out?"

I heard pages rustling, a quiet second of reading, followed by tinny laughter. "Why, no, Ms. James. I'm calling to find out if you'd be interested in joining Love-2-Love, the new online dating service from Robco. We have thousands already entered in the system, and one just may be your soulmate!"

Cripes. I needed a soulmate like a monkey needed a bikini wax. "Yeah, no thanks."

"Registering is free and easy, Ms. James!" he said desperately. He must get paid per rube. "Save yourself from a lifetime of loneliness. Let me read you a testimonial from some of our newest customers."

"Do you know it's 7:30 a.m. in Minnesota?"

"This is from Becky Rafferty, West Virginia: 'Before Love-2-Love, dating was a tedious process that involved many hours of picking through unsavory men in the hopes of finding one good egg. Now Love-2-Love chops that time in half!'"

"Nothing personal," I said. "I know this is your job, but I'm really not interested."

"Check out what *Dr.* Alan Rotis of Pennsylvania had to say: 'Like you, I was suspicious of online dating. That was before I met my beautiful wife, Lora. Thanks, Love-2-Love!'"

I wondered what hellacious karmic debt had placed my name on this phone list. Had I smashed a bunny on my way home from work? Cut off a nun in traffic? Accidentally killed someone? Ooh. Maybe this was payback for passing on the professor I'd been set up with in May. Man, somebody somewhere was keeping a close eye on the score. "I have to go to work."

Another riffling of papers. "I understand, Ms. James. You're happy without love in your life, with no one to take romantic walks with at night or to smile into your eyes as you wake up. Could I give you our web address in case you change your mind and decide you don't want to die alone?"

The second hand on Sunny's wall clock ticked off five beats. "Sure," I said through clenched teeth.

"Do you have pen and paper?"

I clutched my car keys in one hand and the doorknob in the other. "Yup."

"OK, it's www.love2love.com. The two is written as a numeral."

"Got it. Bye."

"Thanks. And rememb—"

I clicked the "End" button, tossed the phone on the couch, let out my calico kitty, Tiger Pop, and Luna, my German Shepherd–mix foster dog, slipped on my shoes, and headed into the day. Nobody likes to be told they're in for a lifetime of loneliness, but for me, the issue was especially painful. I'd officially filed away love in my heart's junk drawer two months ago, right about the time my erstwhile boyfriend, Jeff Wilson, turned up murdered in the Pl–Sca aisle of the Battle Lake library, a bullet hole drilled through his forehead. There was nothing quite like stumbling over your guy's corpse to turn a gal off dating for a spell.

The downside to this out-of-sight, out-of-mind philosophy of mental health and romance was that when I finally found someone worth opening the junk drawer for, it was gonna be messy.

In the meanwhile, I really *was* happy with myself, and it didn't hurt that I had a good detachable showerhead and reliable water pressure. I also was attending a community education class early Saturday mornings taught by Johnny Leeson, local horticultural hottie. The next session was called the "Second Sowings of Lettuce and Beets," but what was more pressing was Johnny's curling dirty-gold hair, strong hands, and his scent of sun-heated black dirt and spicy greens.

Something about his organic quality turned me into an idiot in his presence. That's why I admired him from a distance, keeping my junk drawer tightly closed. When thoughts of Johnny weren't enough to keep me company, I took emotional isolation to a whole new level with Chief Wenonga.

Aah, the Chief.

If *he* had been in the Love-2-Love system, I might have joined.

The Chief visited many a dream, all strong and silent, sporting a full headdress, six-pack abs on a half-naked body, tomahawk in one hand, the other raised in eternal greeting. He was a well-sculpted, strong, and silent alpha male forever guarding the shores of Battle Lake. The Chief was the perfect man, if you overlooked the blatant racist stereotyping.

That, and the fact that he was a twenty-three-foot fiberglass statue.

The Chief, or at least his statue, had been in Battle Lake for two decades this July. The Battle Lake Chamber of Commerce had originally commissioned the figure as a tribute to the flesh-and-blood Chief Wenonga, an Ojibwe leader who'd been on the losing side of the fierce battle against the Dakota that gave the town its name.

The Chief was my favorite part of summering in Battle Lake. At least that's what I'd call what I was doing if I were rich. Really, though, I was house-sitting for my friend Sunny and holding down one job running the Battle Lake Public Library and another as a reporter. The newspaper I worked for, the *Battle Lake Recall*, came out every Monday and sold for fifty cents.

Matter of fact, I'd just gotten promoted and now wrote my own column, Mira's Musings, which was a nice addition to my regular recipe feature, Battle Lake Bites. My "Musings" column ran on the *Recall's* back page. There was even a tiny black-and-white photo of me that ran with it. It was so fuzzy that my long brown hair looked dark gray, my freckled skin looked light gray, and my gray eyes looked black. It didn't really matter because as far as I was concerned, no headshot was going to show my best qualities—my brain and my ass.

I'd been granted Mira's Musings because news seemed to find me in Battle Lake, first in the shape of Jeff, whose lifeless body I'd discovered in the library in May, and then again in June, when I uncovered the mystery of long-ago disappearing jewels on the shore of Whiskey Lake. Ron Sims, *Recall* editor, hadn't asked for any specific content when he assigned me the weekly column ten days ago, but I assumed he wanted me to write about murder and money when I could find them and gossip and garage sales when I couldn't.

It was because of this position as star reporter that I'd been on my way to the final Chief Wenonga Days planning meeting when the telemarketer called. Every July, to celebrate the warrior as well as the coming of his statue a couple hundred years later, Battle Lake hosted a three-day festival. It was scheduled for the weekend closest to the Fourth of July so the town could double-dip on the tourists.

Wenonga Days also included Crazy Days sidewalk sales and a street dance on Friday; more Crazy Days, a kiddie carnival with turtle races, a parade, and fireworks on Saturday; and a bike race, pet and owner look-alike contest, 5K run, and all-town garage sale on Sunday. The revelry planned for this year would be extra special, though, on account of the Chief statue being nearly twenty years old.

The festival happenings weren't in the hands of Battle Lake citizens, however.

Today's Wenonga Days planning meeting was only a formality designed to make the entire town feel involved without letting them actually have any say. Kennie Rogers, Battle Lake's mayor and resident busybody, was the mastermind behind the celebration, and she wanted to keep it that way. Thanks to a tip from my local friend Gina, I knew for a fact that Kennie'd organized the entire weekend last summer, down to personally booking a country group for the street dance and signing up local high school bands and organizations like the Girl Scouts for the parade.

Normally, again according to Gina, Kennie opened the final planning meeting to the public two weeks before Wenonga Days so there was a semblance of town involvement without there being enough time to actually change anything. This year, however, Kennie had been out of town until late yesterday to receive some hush-hush training, and she'd refused to allow the Wenonga Days pretend planning to begin until she returned. I supposed I could have skipped the meeting, particularly because the paper wouldn't come out until Monday, after Wenonga Days was over, but I'd promised Ron I'd cover it.

I sniffed at my armpits as I drove my rusty Toyota Corolla to town and wondered if the unrefined rock deodorant I'd picked up at Meadow Farm Foods outside Fergus was going to hold back the floodgates.

The Channel 7 news, the only station that came in clearly at my double-wide in the woods, was predicting the hottest July in history. The humid, sticky weather made the whole state feel like living inside someone's mouth. It meant people who had to work were cranky, people on vacation were ecstatic, and crops were growing like a house on fire.

Farm mythology declared that if the corn was knee high by the Fourth of July, it'd be a bumper crop. We were two days shy of that date and the corn was already shoulder height on a grown man.

That strangeness should have been a warning to us all.

Chapter 2

No birds sang in the lush hardwoods lining County Road 83. It was too crazy hot. I propped my left foot on the top of my driver's-side door and splayed my blue-painted toenails. The right foot held the gas pedal at a constant sixty-two miles per hour as I navigated the snake curves of Whiskey Road. This was the coolest I was going to get all day.

When I hit Battle Lake, I turned north on Lake Street and drove the two blocks to the library. The yellow brick building was barely ten years old and an incongruity in this tiny town. Roosevelt Everts, a man who made his fortune in the lumber industry and a beloved mainstay in Battle Lake until his death a decade earlier, had bequeathed money from his estate to build it.

The library was located on one corner of Lake and Muskie. The other three corners were occupied by the First National Bank, Lakes Area Dental, and a temporarily abandoned building that once housed Kathy's Klassy Klothes. I'd noticed some activity in the windows of Kathy's Klassy lately, and word on the street was that soon a quilting shop—or maybe a kwilting shop—would occupy the space. Alongside each of these cornerstones were knickknack and antique stores, a bakery, two hardware stores, a drugstore, a post office, a Lutheran church as well as a Baptist one, a surprising assortment of restaurants, a coffee shop, and various service offices—chiropractor, accountant, real estate agent. It was a full-service small town with something for everyone.

I parked my car in the "Librarian's Spot" behind the library and hoofed it the half block to the chamber of commerce office for the planning meeting. The gathering was scheduled to last from eight to ten, but I'd need to ditch early to open the library.

The sun beat down on my dark hair like a blowtorch as I walked, and I wondered if blondes stayed cooler in the summer. By the time I reached the Chamber, sweat droplets tickled my lower back and gathered in the spot where my cleavage would be if there were any fairness in this world. As it was, the sweat trickled to my belly button, unimpeded by my A-cups.

The Chamber shared a squat, one-story brick building with the post office. The main room was designed to hold up to forty people for town meetings, and today, it was full to bursting. I shook my head, amazed that so many townspeople had a stake in the events of Wenonga Days, twentieth anniversary or not. Didn't everyone know the planning wasn't for real? As I threaded my way toward the front of the room, a loud but calm female voice broke through the din.

"I understand that. I'm just saying that to dedicate a town and a weekend to celebrating the objectification and stereotyping of a whole race is a blatant exercise of hegemonic privilege, no matter how much business it brings to Battle Lake."

The people in the crowded room murmured their affront, both at the content and length of her words. I couldn't see the speaker, and I didn't recognize her voice. It had a strange lilt, like she was singing the middle of the sentences. I elbowed closer to get her in view.

"We are *honoring* the Chief." Kennie Rogers was not hard to pick out. She stood at the front of the room, one hand on the podium and the other on her hip. Her clothing was muted, for her: platform flip-flops, black-and-white calfskin capris, a white pleather fringed belt that distracted from her overspill of skin in the thigh/genital area, a suede vest over a yellow tank top not up to the challenge, a peacock-feather choker, what appeared to be tepee earrings, and I swear she wore a beaded headband. She'd curled her brittle, white-blonde hair around it, sort of like a living stage starring her hairline.

Her makeup reinforced her clothes' Indian-stereotype theme—nude lipstick, maroon blush troweled just under her pale cheek apples to imply stark cheekbones, the same color on each side of her nose to make it look fierce, and shades of brown eye shadow caked above her fake eyelashes.

Welcome to Battle Lake.

I jostled some more, still unable to spot the woman who believed it was worth her time to argue about the objectification of Native Americans with a thirty-eight-year-old Norwegian dressed like Porn Pocahontas.

"I recognize that you feel you're honoring the Ojibwe with your festival," the voice broke in.

I finally caught sight of her, standing two rows from the front. She wore a taupe pantsuit. Her strawberry-blonde hair was pulled back in a loose ponytail, revealing a strong-featured, makeup-free face. She looked about my age, late twenties or early thirties, and gave an overall impression of capability. The lines around her generous mouth suggested that her normal facial expression was a smile. This morning, however, she was all grim business. She pushed up her jacket sleeves to continue, and I was surprised by the Celtic tattoos on each of her wrists that belied her otherwise conservative appearance.

"However, to promulgate the stereotype of Indians as savages, to celebrate capitalism with your 'Crazy Days' on what used to be consecrated ground, and to disregard the historical significance of the Battle Lake conflict by offering a kiddie carnival and parade is disrespectful to Native Americans, and to those who respect individual human value." Her words were clipped. I got the impression she was dumbing down her speech for this audience.

Her points ignited a loud buzz throughout the Chamber, but Kennie drowned it out. "What did you say your name was?"

"Dr. Dolores Castle. I am a professor of Native American Studies at the University of Wisconsin, and I represent the People for the Eradication of American-Indian Stereotypes."

PEAS.

I'd always wondered if groups came up with the acronym and then a name to fit it, or vice versa. In this case, I assumed they had concocted the name before the acronym, because that particular vegetable wasn't really associated with crusading strength.

Asparagus I could see. Peas, not so much.

I turned my attention from Dr. Castle to the people watching her. Most wore the Mask of Bewildered Anger, the official expression of rural Minnesotans confronted by liberal progressives. There was no way she understood the depths of institutionalized stereotyping she was up against. Battle Lake even had a tradition of substituting Indian "warriors" (basically Shriners in face paint, fake-leather pants, and moccasins) for clowns at the Wenonga Days parade.

I knew the town wasn't trying to maliciously malign anyone, but I also knew how the celebration might appear to the rest of the world. Battle Lake had only recently replaced the high school mascot, a stereotypical Indian warrior chief they called The Battler, with a bulldog, and that change had been hotly contested.

Dr. Castle continued. "We at PEAS don't want you to stop your festival. We're simply asking that you rename it and remove all Indian caricatures from your region, including Chief Wenonga."

The whispering crowd suddenly went whip-silent.

"Remove . . ." My voice cracked as I went from observer to participant at light speed. Suddenly, she was hitting a little too close to home with this talk about taking my big man away. It slapped me right off my judgmental pedestal. I raised my voice to get her attention. "You mean remove Chief Wenonga *actors* from the *parade*, right?"

She turned to see who'd spoken. "I mean remove the statue of Chief Wenonga from the town."

The room grew hazy as a net of panic encircled me. Then it cleared as I realized the beauty in this idea: *Chief Wenonga could come live with me.* We wouldn't have any misunderstandings about whose job it was to take out the garbage or arguments about my emotional inaccessibility. Oh no. Just clear expectations. He'd be there when I needed him, always.

But then my brain fluttered back to reality. The Chief wasn't mine. If he left Battle Lake, I'd never see him again, and neither would anyone else. Suddenly, the audience erupted with wild talk and outraged looks. Dolores Castle held her ground, hands crossed serenely at her waist.

"Silence!" Battle Lake head of police Gary Wohnt pounded the podium with a gavel he got from I don't know where. The crowd didn't stop talking, but they hushed their voices. Gary had that effect on people. He was big like a bull with dark eyes and hair, and his itchy silences could elicit confessions from the dead. I didn't like him, which made sense: he was pompous, he applied lip balm like his life depended on it, and he always caught me at my worst, usually around dead or seemingly dead bodies.

What I didn't understand was why he didn't like me.

"Are there any other general objections for the Wenonga Days Festival before we move on with the planning?" Gary continued.

I think he meant it as a segue and not a serious inquiry, but to his chagrin, Les Pastner raised his hand. Les was a card-carrying local militia guy. He'd run against Kennie in the last mayoral election on the platform of "Les Is More."

He'd lost.

Les owned the Meat and RV Store right off 210, where he sold used Winnebagos and wild game that he smoked in-house. When business was slow, he worked odd carpentry jobs around town, bitched about the government, and spread rumors that the police left him alone because they knew he would kick their butts if they didn't. Except for running for mayor last summer, he mostly blended in. Apparently, though, Les's activism was cyclical, and we were witnessing his annual blooming.

He stood in the center of the Chamber, atremble in his fatigues, all five foot two inches of him tensed. His close-set features, which'd always made me feel like I was talking to the three finger holes of a bowling ball, appeared more shadowed than usual.

"I been quiet for too long, and I ain't gonna be quiet no more!" Les yelled. His eyes grew disorganized, and I had a moment to wonder if he was really as harmless as I'd always thought.

He puffed himself up, which only served to make his face redder and his features deeper set. "When do we honor the white man? Never, that's when! Nuthin' against the Indians, but it's about time the white man gets some. That's all I'm saying. We need to get rid of Wenonga altogether, replace him with a big white man statue, and have White Man Days in July!" And just like that, Les deflated and stared back at the ground.

The room underwent a collective headshake. Who would have thought anyone had the time to object to a once-a-year festival in a tiny town, and here we had two serious protesters, one of whom was even articulate? This was the last thing I'd expected from the meeting. The ironic part was that Dr. Castle and Les kind of wanted the same thing—no more Wenonga. I considered, as a concession, informing Les that every day was White Man Days in Otter Tail County, but I didn't want to lose my hair in the angry mob scene that'd create.

I scanned the front of the room. Gary Wohnt appeared to be on an inner mental voyage, and Kennie's mouth opened and closed like a landed largemouth bass. Somebody needed to pull this meeting back on track, and soon, because I had to open the library and didn't want to miss the good stuff. I was about to step up when a reedy voice cut through the crowd.

"Bullshit," said Mrs. Berns, my favorite octogenarian, as she wove her way to the front of the room. "You two are singing in the key of crap." She pointed a bony finger at the doctor and then at Les. "As long as we have Chief Wenonga, we're having Wenonga Days, and a twenty-plus-foot statue ain't going nowhere. So stop with the malarkey and get on with the planning. If I don't get back to the home by nine thirty, I don't get my snack."

Mrs. Berns had been a peripheral player in the last two adventures I'd been swept up in. She'd turned out to be a pretty good informant considering she lived in the Senior Sunset, the local nursing home and not exactly what you'd think would be a hotbed for clues. Turned out the old-homers had the best dirt in town. Sometime last month, Mrs. Berns had also created and then applied for an assistant librarian position at the library, and she was making me proud I'd hired her. Despite a randy streak that often found her dancing suggestively and wearing see-through blouses with no bra, she was a good worker and a practical woman, which was my favorite kind.

Mrs. Berns's interjection yanked Kennie out of her reverie and back into her denial mode. She clapped her hands as if she were waking us all from a dream. "It's time to plan a party!" PEAS, Les, and all things unhappy were dismissed. Reality got in line behind Kennie.

That was my cue to leave. I cut out, hurrying up the street to unlock the library and get to work, fantasizing about Chief Wenonga the whole way.

Chapter 3

Surprisingly, I enjoyed my job. If you'd asked me when I was a girl what I wanted to do when I grew up, I wouldn't have said "manage a library." Actually, I probably would've said "cat," but I've always been a dreamer. Currently, I lacked the degree and the skills to be a legitimate librarian, but under the circumstances, the town was happy to have me. And I was pleased to be here, mostly.

The library perfectly joined my loves of books and organization.

I liked the job less on days like today, however. My shift was a whirlwind of clearing out paperwork, answering a mad influx of tourists' questions ("If I like Janet Evanovich, who else would I like?" "Can I check out the magazines?" "Do you give library cards to out-of-towners?" "Where would I find that purple children's book about the bear?"), and shelving books, leaving me no time to draft Mira's Musings or write my recipe column or even find out what came of the morning's uproar at the Chamber. In fact, I was forced to stay late to catch up on my daily paperwork and didn't leave the library until 8:00 p.m.

When I stepped outside the air-conditioned chambers, the hot, muggy air hit me like a blast from a kiln. My hair immediately skull-capped me, and my last bit of energy was broiled off. The blacktop parking lot felt soft and sticky and reeked of cooked gravel and blistering motor oil as I walked to my car. I was smart enough to pull my tank top over my hand before grabbing the metal door handle. Once in, I rolled down all four windows, moved the emergency blanket to cover the volcanic pleather that was the front seat, cranked the radio, and headed for home.

When I pulled up to the mailbox at the end of my mile-long drive-way seven minutes later, I realized I was too tired to eat, forget about calling around to find out the end result of the pretend planning meet-ing. I parked the car in the shade of the lilac bushes, near where both Luna and Tiger Pop were sprawled in the grass. Luna thumped her tail and Tiger Pop opened one eye when I petted her, but that was about all the welcome home I got.

In hand I had a bill from Lake Region Electric; a flyer for a new store called Elk Meat Etc. opening in Clitherall, the tiny dot of a town six miles east of Battle Lake; and a birthday card–size white envelope. My birthday had been in May, and only one person I knew sent cards two months late: my mom. My heart flip-flopped. There was no return address, but the post office stamp said "Paynesville."

Yep, it was from my mom.

I thought about opening it, but decided I wasn't up for it tonight. I loved my mom, but our relationship wasn't easy. We'd had a minor breakthrough since I'd moved to Battle Lake, but I was treading lightly. I think I was still mad at her for not divorcing my dad when she had the chance.

She'd stayed married to him despite his drunkenness, until he was involved in a fatal car accident at the end of my junior year. After that, I was known as Manslaughter Mark's daughter and fled to the Twin Cities as soon as I had my high school diploma. That worked out for a while, until I started doing my best imitation of my dad, getting drunk every night and letting my life slide. Moving to Battle Lake had been designed to redirect me, and I was proud of how I'd been doing since May.

At least I was until I received the letter from Dr. Bundy last month, asking me to return to Minneapolis to be his research assistant in the U of M's English Department. When I read that letter, I sort of felt like a failure, spinning my wheels in a small town while life and a real career passed me by. So I didn't read it very often, though in the back of my brain I knew I'd need to make a decision about staying in Battle Lake or moving back to Minneapolis by the end of this month, as he'd requested.

I dropped my unopened mail on the table inside the front door, changed Tiger Pop's and Luna's water, cracked some ice cubes into their bowls, refilled their food, coaxed them into the stifling house, and apologized for neglecting them all day. They both plopped down on the cool linoleum near the refrigerator. I considered joining them. The ant creeping across the floor nixed that idea. I tossed my sticky clothes over the back of the couch and crawled naked onto my bed, a fan pointing at my head. The air it was moving around was so scorching that I would have been better off rigging up a flamethrower.

I slept on top of the sheets, except for my feet, which I always covered in bed. Seeing a *Roots* rerun on TV as a child had affected me to the point where I couldn't leave my feet vulnerable for fear of having them chopped off as I slept. I knew the sheets wouldn't stop an axe, but they made me feel safer, and after two months in Battle Lake, I needed all the reassurance I could get.

At least I could fall asleep knowing I wouldn't be discovering another dead body.

Finding three corpses in as many months would be *banana pants*.

Chapter 4

I woke up with a layer of sweat covering me like a salty wool blanket. After an icy shower and a quick breakfast of whole-grain Total with organic raisins, I was on my early way to meet another oppressively hot day. My outdoor thermometer read seventy-eight degrees, and it wasn't even seven.

I knew my Mira's Musings column was going to be somehow related to yesterday's Wenonga Days planning meeting, so I needed to find out how it had ended and get a draft out before I opened the library. Besides my regular filing, ordering, and organizing duties there, I wanted to chase down some grant funding and work on my latest banned books display. (Those puppies flew off the shelves.) Somewhere in there I also needed to find a recipe "representative of Battle Lake"—in Ron Sims's words—for that column. My to-do list for the day was buzzing like a kicked hornet's nest.

The fertile smell of the swamp I passed tickled my nose, and I could hear frogs singing in the sloughs. It was a peaceful time to be out in the world. The sun was flexing its lavender-lemon arms over the horizon when I turned right onto County Road 78, just up the street from the Shoreline Restaurant and Chief Wenonga. I'd chosen this route because driving past the Chief on this gonna-be-busy day seemed like a natural way to get my (mental) juices flowing.

I'd just turned onto the blacktop when a red tank zoomed over the hill and aggressively hugged my bumper. Whoever it was had their high beams on, unnecessary in the bright dawn and making it impossible for me to see their face in my rearview mirror. I was pretty sure it was a guy with a small penis, though.

My feet twitched to tap my brakes, but it was too early in the morning to trade my safety for pride. I pulled to the right to let the Hummer pass and glared at the silver-rimmed tires as they raced by me and my puddle jumper. Feeling cranky, I drove the last mile into town, cursing tourists and gas-guzzling army vehicles driven by civilians. I was moving on to getting mad at the color red when I crested the hill right before the Shoreline.

The restaurant's parking lot was peppered with a sprinkling of early-morning fishers in town for the excellent eggs Benedict and hash browns. My temper cooled as I thought of yummy breakfast food and the fact that I was just about to say a great good morning to my big fiberglass man.

I leaned forward in my seat so I could spot Chief Wenonga a millisecond sooner. Just beyond the Shoreline's brown roof, I made out his concrete base, with four enormous bolts poured into it.

Hmmm. I didn't remember noticing the bolts before.

A beat later, I realized why.

The bolts held Chief Wenonga up, one each embedded in the front and back of his feet. Now that he was no longer there, the bolts were obvious.

My gut clenched in horror as my brain realized what had happened. *Someone had kidnapped Chief Wenonga.*

Chapter 5

I screeched into the parking lot, threw myself out of the car, and ran to the Chief's concrete base. I touched the four bolts, cool and wet with morning dew, and stared around frantically. Where were the police? Where was the ambulance? Why wasn't anyone *doing* anything?

The fishers were visible through the picture windows of the Shoreline, tucking into their eggs, their eyes happy, as if someone important to us hadn't just been abducted. Cars drove past leisurely on 78. Waves lapped at the shore of Battle Lake, and the sun rose steadily. I wanted to pull out my hair. How could the world go on as if nothing was wrong? I was struck with an image of me slapping the Chief's photo on the back of milk cartons and attaching posters to interstate semis.

Mira, control yourself.

I swallowed a lump of paste and squeezed my hands into fists. I took three deep breaths. There must be a rational explanation for this. People didn't *kidnap* ginormous fiberglass statues. Probably at the meeting yesterday it'd been decided that the Chief needed a cleaning, and workers had quickly driven him to some fiberglass statue detailing shop. Or maybe they'd decided to add a "Find the Chief" contest to Wenonga Days. Or maybe . . . an icy finger traced a shiver down my spine. Maybe, just maybe, Les had decided to do his own part to promote White Man Days, or PEAS was pulling a stunt of PETA proportions.

My horror turned to anger, and then, thank god, to embarrassment. My Chief Wenonga obsession had clearly gotten out of hand. I made a mental note to find a new, more reliable fixation, and in the meanwhile, to visit the local coffee shop, the Fortune Café, to see what I could find out about the Chief's new location. I wiped my dew-covered hands on my shorts and marched back toward my car. When I reached for the door latch, a swath of red caught my eye. It was on my faded cutoffs, and it was the smear I'd just left with my hand.

Since when was dew red?

For a moment, I entertained the notion that the Chief had bled when he was removed from his posts. It made sense, in Upside Down World—the posts were the only things I'd touched. It was the fiberglass stigmata.

Then good sense crept into my head, followed immediately by fear, and they both slid down my neck and back like cold oil.

I had real blood on my hands.

Chapter 6

My legs propelled me back to the concrete stand, and bending down on shaky knees, I examined the bloody post more closely in the hazy, hot morning sunlight. I saw what I'd missed earlier in the throes of my Chief grief. At the base of the post was a gory patch of dark hair the size of a silver dollar, still adhering to the chunk of scalp it'd sprouted from. Where, I wondered, was the rest of the person? It was time for the law. I hurried to my car and screeched the mile to the police station.

It was a Friday morning on a major holiday weekend, and I was sure the local police department would be open for business. I was wrong. There were no Crown Vics parked out front, and Wohnt's customized blue-and-white Jeep was nowhere in sight. A quick peek in the door confirmed that the place was empty. I could always call 911, but I needed to figure out how to report a chunk of a scalp next to a missing fiberglass Native American without sounding unhinged.

A quick review of the facts verified that would be impossible, so I drove to the public phone outside Battle Lake Gas to make the call, nervous because I'd never dialed 911 before. It felt like an audition.

"911. What is your emergency?"

"Umm. I'm in Battle Lake, and we have a big statue here, Chief Wenonga? Well, he's missing, and there's blood on the posts that held him up, and it looks like there's some hair and skin there, too."

"Human hair?"

What, was I Dr. Quinn, Medicine Woman now? "Looked like."

"What is the location of the blood and hair?"

"Right off of Lake Street in Battle Lake, on the other side of town if you're coming in from the south. Next to the Shoreline Restaurant in Halverson Park."

"Are you at that site right now?"

I suddenly felt the uneasy tickle of being watched. I glanced around and spotted a handful of cars driving past on 78 and, on the other side of that, Timmy Christianson shaking out the rugs inside the door of Larry's Grocery. Immediately behind me and on the other side of the front glass window, the Battle Lake Gas clerk was reading *The National Enquirer* and smoking Pall Malls. "No."

"Your name?"

"Linda Luckerman." The lie came quickly. If I'd learned anything from my stint in Battle Lake, it was that you don't look for trouble, because it'll find you just fine on its own, *thankyouverymuch*.

"We'll send a car right out. Can you be waiting for us at the site?"

"You betcha." Lie number two.

"Thank you, Ms. Luckerman." Click.

When I replaced the phone, I was revolted to see a line of blood crusting my hand. Now that I was removed from the visual horror of the scalp, I was convinced that it was human. The hair attached to it had been thinning, about two inches long, and even though the edges were gory with blood, I could see it'd been recently trimmed.

I stepped inside the air-conditioned gas station to wash my hands, scrub the front of my shorts, and buy a Nut Goodie, in that order. I needed to clear my head.

The true terror of what I'd just seen didn't begin to sink in until I paid for and palmed the candy. I slipped around the side of the building to chow it while sitting on my haunches, out of sight. As the creamy chocolate and nuts slid down my throat, it became immediately apparent that I needed to hightail it out of the Battle Lake Gas parking lot because my 911 call could be traced. When I bit into the hummingbird-food-sweet maple center, it also occurred to me that it wouldn't hurt to wipe my bloody prints off the phone on my way out.

I sneaked back around to the gas pumps, eyed the clerk, who was still reading *The Enquirer* with his back to me, yanked some paper towels from the dispenser, and surreptitiously scrubbed the pay phone's handset and number pad. I chucked the last piece of chocolate into my mouth and the green, red, and white wrapper into the garbage and decided to amble down to the Fortune Café and drink some coffee as if nothing were amiss. Best way to gather clues. It was still entirely possible that the Chief's disappearance was unrelated to the bloody scalp at his base, and if I kept my mouth shut, I could find out what'd happened without looking like a dum-dum.

The Fortune was across the street, a block and a half down from the library. Sid and Nancy, the owners, had moved to Battle Lake from the Cities and bought and renovated the charming Victorian-style dwelling a few years earlier. The downstairs housed a full-service bakery and coffee shop made up of four rooms—the large, flour-dusted kitchen; the main dining room, where you placed your order and could sit at one of five large tables; the bathroom with a hand-lettered, wooden SHIT OR GET OFF THE POT sign inside; and a smaller all-purpose room off the main one that held couches, bookshelves filled with mystery and romance paperbacks and some nonfiction, two desktop computers with internet access, and board games like Scrabble and Monopoly. The sprawling upstairs was Sid and Nancy's home.

The welcoming jingle of the door and the aromatic wash of fresh-roasted coffee and candied-ginger scones called up a Pavlovian response. I found myself relaxing, even downgrading the Chief and the human scalp from "scary urgent" to "worrisome" as I glided to the front counter, nodding at the handful of patrons I knew.

"Green tea or decaf mocha, Mira?"

Sid had forgone her usual flannel shirt in favor of a camo-green tank top, and she was growing out her mullet into a softer, feathered bob. I didn't know what was at the source of her style changes, but I thought it might have had something to do with all the issues of *Cosmo* she'd been reading at the library lately.

"Today's a straight mocha kinda morning, Sid. Do you have any bagels left?"

She winked. "For you, we have bagels. Onion or honey oat?"

"Honey oat with olive cream cheese, please." It was feeling like a two-breakfast day. I fiddled casually with the plastic-flower-topped pens at the front counter, all seven of them stabbed deep into a flowerpot of French-roast coffee beans. "So, any news in town?"

Sid smirked. "Do you mean the hullabaloo at the planning meeting yesterday? Nancy and I are thinking of naming a new drink after Les. We'll call it the White Man."

"What's in it?"

"Milk, with a side of fish-shaped sugar cookies." Her smirk turned into a wicked grin. "Or whatever you want. It's Battle Lake."

"You hear any other buzz?"

She waggled her brows. "Just the hum of your thighs as tomorrow's community ed class looms large. When are you going to ask that Johnny Leeson out, anyhow?"

That set me back a step. Rumors traveled fast as greased ice in a small town, but I'd confided in only my friend Gina about my crush on Johnny, Battle Lake's resident hot, hot hottie. If everyone knew I had a hankering for him, did that also mean they knew about my fixation on Chief Wenonga? I shrugged evasively, traded Sid a five for the bagel and coffee, and headed to a computer. I set myself up at the Dell with a direct sight line to the front door.

My plan was to fake researching my next recipe while keeping one ear on the talk. All the important news came through the Fortune, and I'd soon be able to find out what was up at Halverson Park, former residence of one Chief Wenonga. My favorite pretend work was recipe hunting for my column, so I dug in, hoping the clicking of the keyboard would soothe me. Mostly I relied on internet searches using the key words "weird recipes."

I fired up the computer and sipped my chocolate coffee, cinnamon-laced whipped cream sticking to my upper lip.

Today, I varied my search by entering "weird *Midwest* recipes." The first hit was for french-fried skunk. What got me about this so-called recipe was all its assumptions—that a person could get their hands on two dead skunks, know how to skin and debone them, and successfully remove the scent glands before slicing the little carnivores into "french fry–shaped" pieces. After that, it was a pretty straightforward fried-food recipe, except that you needed to boil the skunk for forty minutes and ladle off the scum before plopping the pieces in an egg, milk, and flour shake. Then, voilà! You were ready to fry.

It occurred to me that I didn't want to offer up a recipe that had everyone in town making noodles at midnight, so I kept searching. Just like that, the magic instructions splashed onto my computer screen: "Find a Man Casserole." The ingredients were tried-and-true. Two cans cream of mushroom soup, half a box of elbow macaroni, half a cup of milk, a can of tuna (the better to bait your man with, I imagined), one can of green beans, and half a cup of pearl onions. Boil the macaroni until soft, drain, and then bake the whole works at 375 degrees for fifty minutes, pull out, cover in a fish scale pattern with whole, plain, non-ruffled potato chips, and cook for another five minutes or until the chips are browned.

This town was missing one giant man and most of another, smaller one, and maybe, just maybe, if all of Battle Lake cooked this casserole the same night, we'd find the Chief and the guy-mi-nus-a-chunk-of-scalp who'd disappeared with him. If nothing else, it would offer the locals some variety from fried panfish and frozen pizza.

I was emailing a copy of this recipe to Ron and enjoying the calm feeling I got when I finished a job when the door to the café crashed open. In fell a red-faced Jedediah Heike, son of the owners of the Last Resort, a charming getaway on the north side of town.

Jed was an amiable stoner in his early twenties, medium height with stringy arms and legs swinging off his skinny body, his happy head topped off with a mop of curly brown hair. He'd befriended me when I moved to town in April and was overall a sweet and harmless guy, if not the brightest light in the harbor. I foresaw him living with his parents his entire life, a regular Battle Lake fixture.

"Chief Wenonga is gone!" he yelled.

I groaned. *Of all the people to spread the news.* Because Jed spent most of his time smiling and nodding, he wasn't exactly the poster child for credibility. Even more awful? Now I had to accept the worst. I swallowed past the gummy ball that had just formed in my throat.

The Chief had been stolen.

Sid raced out from the back room, wiping her hands on a cloth. "What's that, Jed? Are you OK?"

"The Chief Wenonga statue," he cried. "It's missing. It's gone!"

Sid frowned. "You ever hear about the little boy who cried wolf, Jeddy?"

The handful of patrons in the café laughed good-naturedly, but Jed's face fell. His brown doe eyes landed hopefully on me.

I sighed and stood up, walking into the main room. "It's true. I drove by there this morning. Chief Wenonga is gone."

Jed grinned like he'd just discovered a fresh, whole Dorito in the crack of his recliner.

"Why didn't you say anything?" Sid asked me. Nancy came up behind and put her arm around her partner.

I shrugged, feigning innocence. "I thought they took it as part of the Chief Wenonga Days deal. You think we should call someone?"

"Ja!" Sid reverted to a good Norwegian brogue in times of stress. She dialed the Battle Lake Police Department, got through to someone, and in minutes, a Crown Vic sped past, siren blaring. I didn't know if they were responding to my 911 or Sid's call, but the results were the same.

Most of the café customers had filed onto the street by this time, gawking in the direction of the Shoreline. I shut down my computer, bundled up my uneaten bagel in a napkin, and jogged down the road. There was safety in numbers, and now I could snoop up close while half the town milled around.

Besides, I wanted to be there when Gary Wohnt discovered that somebody had stolen a twenty-three-foot heirloom on his watch.

Chapter 7

Jed tagged along behind me. I tried to ignore the huffing and puffing caused by his ganja-restricted lungs, but when he started to suck in air like a vacuum with a hole in its bag, I slowed my sprint to a fast walk. I was dying to reach the scene of the crime in time to hear what the police made of the scalp, but not at the expense of Jed's lungs.

"I bet some kids stole the Chief." *Wheeze.*

"Maybe. You OK?"

He tried to puff himself up but quickly realized he needed the air elsewhere. He opted instead to run his hand through his sweaty curls. His black Phish T-shirt was plastered to his scrawny chest. It was still morning, and already it felt like hell's kitchen.

"Oh, ja. I'm fine." *Wheeze.* "I had a feeling something like this was gonna happen. There's street gangs forming in town."

We were coming down the hill. West Battle Lake glittered in the hot morning sun to our right, and Halverson Park sat on our left. Gary Wohnt leaned on his open Jeep door, radio in hand. I could hear the rumble of his voice, but we were too far away to make out his words. "Where'd you hear about gangs?"

Jed hitched up his belt and pulled a pack of Jolly Ranchers from his back pocket. He offered me a watermelon one and popped it in his mouth when I shook my head. "I'm not sure where. You know, I might just be thinking of a movie I saw. It's hard to keep that stuff straight."

I patted his arm. Jed was so transparently dorky that it was impossible not to love him. "You want to go talk to Wohnt with me?"

Jed's face went white except for the bong-shaped ring of acne around his mouth. "Nah. You go on ahead."

I smiled at his back as he disappeared into the crowd, his shoulders hunched around his ears to make himself less visible. I strolled to Wohnt's car, reaching it just as he clicked off the radio.

"Secure area, Ms. James," he barked.

"Need help putting up the police tape?"

His Poncherello-style reflective sunglasses were impenetrable as he grabbed the yellow tape from his trunk and strung it around the elm trees circling the Chief's former position. The empty stand the Chief had stood proudly on for a couple of decades poked up like a tombstone.

We'd lost our leader.

In this part of the state, erecting twenty-three feet of kitsch to honor a person, event, or creature was not out of the ordinary. In fact, if a person happened to be cruising around in space and looked down at Earth, and if the only discernible shapes from that distance were continents, oceans, and gargantuan statues, Battle Lake and its environs would stand out like a redneck Stonehenge.

There was a reason so many statues ended up in the area, and it was called tourism. The population of any Minnesota town situated near a lake (which was every Minnesota town) swelled in the summer as hordes of men came to fish and drink, long-suffering women came to shop and drink, and kids came because they had no choice. That built-in audience served as the perfect justification for creating oversize replicas of everyday phenomena, a dioramic playground for Bob's Big Boy's fiberglass family.

The tiny town of Battle Lake, population 747, had more to offer than Chief Wenonga, of course—there were the walleye honey spots, antique shops, an ice cream and candy parlor, cozy resorts, and bait stores—but it was its position at the center of a maelstrom of strange effigies that made it the crème de la crème of tourist stops. Oh yes. The glorious and disturbingly sexy twenty-three-foot fiberglass statue of the Chief was just the beginning. Eighteen miles to the west of the Chief lay the town of Ashby, where an Olympic-size coot overlooked Pelican Lake. The ten-foot-tall concrete mud hen was so heavy that the wings had to be supported by a metal brace.

Fifteen miles to the west and north of the coot sat Fergus Falls, where the world's biggest otter kept an eye on the shore of Grotto Lake. He was forty feet long from his black nose to his rump of pure poured concrete. Vergas was farther east and served as the residence of a twenty-foot-tall loon. North of that was the world's largest turkey, twenty-two feet of fowl fiberglass, in Frazee.

South and east, in the town of Ottertail, rested the biggest dragonfly in the universe. If you followed the back roads farther south, you'd end up in Alexandria, where you could get your picture taken between the welcoming fiberglass thighs of Ole Oppe, better known as Big Ole. Though he had five feet on Chief Wenonga, I think the Chief could take him in a fair fight. Driving northwest back toward Battle Lake through Vining, you would find everyday objects rendered colossal in scrap metal along Highway 210—a huge clothespin, a titanic toe, a supersize square knot.

There was more, but you get the idea.

Every bit of this deranged splendor was flaunted in or within sixty miles of Battle Lake, situated in Otter Tail County in west central Minnesota, a land unto itself where there was one boat for every six residents. My three months living here had proven that Otter Tail County had all the makings of a Midwestern Bermuda Triangle, and the fact that Chief Wenonga had gone missing just underscored that notion.

By the time Gary Wohnt had come full circle with the yellow-and-black tape, two more police cruisers had pulled up, one county and one Battle Lake. Kennie Rogers rode in the back of the Battle Lake car, behind the cage. When the driver failed to let her out immediately, she began pounding on the inside of her window. The crowd chuckled but had the sense to do it facing away from her.

"For heaven's sake, didn't your mama raise you right?" Kennie demanded of the young officer, once she was released. Her vaguely southern accent was eternally puzzling, given that she'd been born in Battle Lake and had moved out of town for only two semesters right after high school to get her cosmetology degree from Alexandria Technical College, all of forty-five miles away.

The offending officer, a baby-faced newcomer named Miller, steadied Kennie by her elbow as she adjusted her patriotic stovepipe hat, which rode three inches taller than the crowd. It did a lovely job of accenting her glittering, roaring twenties–style red, white, and blue can-can dress with metallic fringe. The dress itself was cute, if completely out of place and several sizes too small for Kennie.

She ducked her flustered, patriotic body under the crime scene tape and marched right up to Gary Wohnt.

I was at the front of the crowd and heard every word they said.

"What in the hell is going on here?"

Gary Wohnt fished a tiny black, white, and yellow tub of lip balm out of his front shirt pocket and twisted off the top. He frosted his lips like they were devil's food cake before answering her. When finished, he said simply, "Wenonga is gone."

"And I'm not stupid." She tucked a stray lock of hair beneath the stovepipe hat. "Now that the introductions are over, why don't you tell me what the devil happened?"

An Otter Tail County officer approached them, a 35 mm camera strapped around his neck, and slipped a latex glove onto each hand. "Chief Wohnt, Ms. Rogers." He nodded and proceeded to the statue's base.

"You know Brando's supposed to be here any minute," Kennie hissed to Wohnt. "And you pulled me out of rehearsal for this?"

My ears perked up. Brando as in a relative of *Marlon* Brando? And what sort of rehearsal had Kennie been at, wearing that outfit?

"I know," Wohnt said calmly. He capped the lip balm and slipped it back into his pocket.

Kennie threw up her hands in exasperation, nearly knocking off her Uncle Sam hat. She stormed over to the county officer, who was photographing the post where I'd spotted the scalp earlier.

"What are you taking pictures of?" she asked, her voice sweet like honey.

"Ms. Rogers, I'm going to have to ask you to leave the secured area," he said, raising his hand to signal to the Battle Lake officer. "Miller? Will you please escort Ms. Rogers beyond the perimeter? And grab the fingerprinting kit from the back seat of my car. I've got a beautiful set here."

The crowd was buzzing behind me, but I couldn't hear it over the sound of my stomach crashing to the pavement. That beautiful set of fingerprints had to be mine.

Boy, had I stepped right into it again.

Chapter 8

I was ready to throw up.

If they discovered my fingerprints mixed in with the blood on Wenonga's concrete base, I was guaranteed top billing as the prime suspect in whatever statue-stealing, man-scalping extravaganza had taken place. And I knew from experience that the local law would *not* be sympathetic to my case. I could confess to Gary right now about touching one of the posts, but the fact that I hadn't told him right away would appear highly suspicious.

I threaded my way through the crowd, trying to put distance between the cops and me, and ran smack-dab into Dr. Castle. Today she was dressed in conservative espadrilles, an ankle-length peasant skirt in muted browns, and a beige silk tank top. Her hair was pulled back into a bun, and her face was pale except for the sunburned tip of her nose.

"Whoa," she said, her eyes kind as she stepped back a pace. "See something up there you didn't like?"

I smiled weakly. "I think I ate a bad breakfast."

She nodded sympathetically. "I saw you at the town hall meeting yesterday, right?"

"Me, and a bunch of angry citizens." I tossed a glance over my shoulder. "I guess you got your wish about Chief Wenonga."

She studied the space where his head used to be. "They know who did it?"

Her eyes were a light green, almost translucent, and this close, I could see the dusting of freckles over her cheeks and peeling nose. I turned back to glance the same direction she was. The police didn't know who'd taken the Chief, but I knew who *hadn't*—me. I also knew who would gain from doing it: Dr. Castle and Les Pastner. Since it was in my best interest to pin that guilty tail to a donkey other than myself and fast, I'd best start asking questions. I swallowed my unease and held out my hand.

"Not that I heard. I'm Mira James, by the way." Castle shook my proffered hand, warmly and confidently, as I continued. "I work for the *Battle Lake Recall*. Mind if I buy you a beer tonight and pick your brain for an article I'm working on about Wenonga Days?" I winced at my word choice, remembering too late that there might be a little brain on the Wenonga base.

"Sure. Like we say in PEAS, all press is good press."

"How about the Rusty Nail at seven?" I said. "It's right on Lake Street, a block or so down from Stub's."

"It's a plan." She smiled and moved toward the front just as Jed found me.

"This is wild stuff, Mira." His normally bloodshot eyes were glowing, and the sun had dried the sweat from his curls, making them wild. "I heard one cop say there was a chunk of head on the post. Someone got *scalped!*"

"Mm-hmm." I tuned him out as I wondered how I could find out what Les Pastner, my other suspect, had been up to last night. It wouldn't be easy. As far as I knew, outside of work, the man kept to himself. He lived in the woods in a two-room house he'd built by hand. It was basically a glorified shed, and except for his mangy dog, he was alone out there. He occasionally visited the library to check out books on tracking animals, the French Revolution, and bombs, but we'd never conversed in depth. I'd witnessed him once or twice riding a good rant at Bonnie & Clyde's, one of two bars in Clitherall, so I knew that he'd talk if the right buttons were pressed.

I just needed to figure out what those buttons were.

Jed interrupted my thoughts. "You hear what everyone's saying? People think Wenonga's ghost came back to haunt us all." He laughed and grabbed another Jolly Rancher. Grape. "Hey, Mir. Wanna have supper tonight? Say, the Rusty Nail at six? I was supposed to meet up with some people to go to the street dance later, but you could hang out with us."

"Sure, Jed. Whatever." I scanned the crowd for Les, searching for his telltale greasy gray hair and fatigues, but there were too many people gawking and I wasn't tall enough to see over most of their heads.

"Great! I'll pick you up."

"What?" I was still searching the crowd.

"For supper and the dance tonight. I'll pick you up at six."

I replayed our conversation in my head. *Dang.* "No, sorry, I'll have to meet you at the Nail. I have other plans later."

He appeared slightly dejected, or maybe it was just the exertion of our sprint up the block and the Jolly Ranchers catching up with him. "Cool."

"Cool." I smiled at Jed, who really was harmless, and moved on. As I looped my way through the crowd, I puzzled over who this Brando person was that Kennie had referred to, and why he'd care about the missing Chief Wenonga. Although it was against my better judgment, my survival instinct, and actually every fiber of my being, I decided to go to the source to find out more.

Thanks to her towering hat, she was not hard to locate. I found her near Wohnt's vehicle.

"Kennie?" I said, when I was within speaking distance.

She glared down her nose at me, a few inches taller even in her star-spangled ballet slippers. "Hello, Mira. It looks like we've got ourselves another mystery. Are you on the case?"

Did waiting to be named the prime suspect count? "It's pure coincidence that I'm here, though I'd sure like to get the Chief back in time for the Wenonga Days kickoff tonight." I played it casual, hooking my thumbs in my front pockets and leaning back on my heels. "Was that Brando person you were talking about part of the entertainment?"

For a second, I thought she was going to ignore me. She probably still felt slighted for being booted from the secured area. Then, in her haughtiest voice, she straightened her red, white, and blue hat and said, "Brando Erikkson is an *artist*. He and his company, Fibertastic Enterprises, created the Chief." Her voice was raising, and the spangles on her dress started shivering like pebbles before an earthquake. "Do you hear me? The man who created Chief Wenonga is on his way here, and we have lost the Chief! *We* have *lost* him!"

Kennie was working herself into a lather, and Lord knows where that would have gone if Mrs. Berns hadn't walked by just then in her flower-patterned housedress and muttered, "You look like ten pounds of shit in a five-pound bag, Rogers."

Immediately, Kennie was back to her Plasticine self. "And a good day to you, too, Mrs. Berns. I can count on your help with the Fourth of July parade cleanup, right?"

Mrs. Berns snorted and kept walking. "I'd rather sanitize a public restroom with my tongue."

And with that, Mrs. Berns was swallowed up by the crowd. I decided to copy her disappearing act and slunk away after a quick thank-you to Kennie. If I beat cheeks, I could maybe track down Les before he opened his store and ask him a few questions in private. That weird little militia guy might be the only thing between me and some uncomfortably long jail time.

Not a reassuring thought.

Chapter 9

Despite its grand name, the Meat and RV Store was just an unassuming brown building off County Road 210. If not for the enormous red-lettered sign featuring a madly grinning sausage driving a Winnebago, it would be easy to miss. My Toyota was dwarfed by the five used RVs in the parking lot, every one of which had seen better days. A quick scan of the building's front revealed no light or movement inside, and when I jogged around back, I saw no sign of Les's battered Ford pickup. A quick pull at the rear door revealed that it was locked, and no one answered when I knocked.

Unfortunately, there was nothing to do but head to the library. Maybe I could catch Les on my lunch break. I could almost hear the clock ticking as I headed to work, me racing against the fingerprinting evidence.

Time was not on my side.

I was a half an hour early opening the library, and Mrs. Berns was a half an hour late. She showed up with a group of elderly friends, who were all tittering about the missing statue, the upcoming Fourth of July parade, and Kennie's surprise guest. The smell of pressed powder and Bengay menthol hovered over them like a cloud.

"I hear Mayor Kennie has invited Marlon Brando to town!" Ida said. She was one of my favorite old ladies in the world, and Battle Lake had a pretty nice selection. She always looked snappy, and today was no exception. Her hair was a crisp white, cut short, and still in the shape of the curlers she'd slept in. She wore a wrinkle-free yellow polo shirt with the collar neatly ironed, orange shorts with a crease in the front, and brown bobby socks with her white Keds.

"Naw, it's Bronson Pinchot," Mrs. Berns said. I hadn't noticed her flip-flops back at Halverson Park and saw that her pink toenails complemented her flowered housedress nicely.

"The guy from *Perfect Strangers*?" Ida asked.

"You sure it's not Charles Bronson coming to town? I heard Charles Bronson." This from Ida's shy sister, Freda. She was dressed almost identical to her sister, except the colors and creases weren't as crisp.

I shook my head. This was how rumors started. I set Mrs. Berns to the task of reshelving the returned books, waved at her coterie as it old-lady-shuffled out of the building, and got to work on a rough draft of my Mira's Musings column. Given the recent happenings, I decided to title it **It's My Party, and I'll Fly if I Want To:**

> In a bizarre turn of events, the Chief Wenonga statue has disappeared from Battle Lake just as the plans for his twentieth birthday party were getting underway. Police on the Halverson Park scene Friday morning found only an empty base, with the four posts that supported the statue coated with what appeared to be blood.
>
> The police currently have no leads, and this reporter for sure didn't do it.
>
> The town of Battle Lake is hoping the Chief is returned home for his holiday. If you have any idea what happened to the Chief, please email me at miraj@prtel.com or contact the Battle Lake Police Department.

I crossed out the middle paragraph and chewed on the end of a pen. I realized I wanted to do more than just write my column. I wanted to cover all of Wenonga Days, now that it was Wenonga-less and my ass might be grass. I phoned my editor to get the go-ahead.

"Hey, Ron. How's tricks?"

Ron Sims was a paunchy, grouchy, warmhearted man who was fortified in life by his dedication to journalism and drive to publicly make out with his wife. I didn't know if the latter was a fetish so much as a habit at this point, but if you got Ron and Rhoda together, they sprayed each other like cats in heat. Their affection was both inspiring and stomach churning.

"You got my article, James?"

"Absolutely. Just typed it up." I was running spell-check as I spoke. "I have a scoop, though."

"Scoop this. Chief Wenonga disappeared, and we have half the state arriving to town for his party today."

"I know." No spelling errors. "I might have an idea where he's gone, but I need to cover the whole weekend. Let me be your Wenonga Days go-to gal," I pleaded.

There were a few beats of silence as he considered, or as he frenched his wife. Hard to know over the phone. "You got until Monday to get me 1,500 words," he finally said. "I want at least three different articles."

"Thanks, Ron!"

"Yup." Click.

I was just about to call Mrs. Berns over to cover the front while I used the bathroom when I spotted Battle Lake police chief Gary Wohnt striding toward the library's front glass doors, his shiny lips and fathomless sunglasses reflecting light as sharp as arrows.

Christ as a cracker.

Chapter 10

I couldn't draw in a full breath. Had they matched my fingerprints so quickly? My too-short life of freedom flashed through my brain. I imagined myself in my garden, soaking up the sun; playing fetch with Luna and being ignored by Tiger Pop; swimming in Whiskey Lake's cool waters just out my front door; eating recognizable food and not showering with strangers.

That last one settled it.

I couldn't go to jail.

I dropped to the ground and wedged my body into one of the larger open-faced cupboards that made up the library's tall front counter. Wohnt would need to pass through the "Employees Only" gate at the far side to find me, and I was gambling that he wouldn't.

The door donged open, followed by a rapping on the desk above me, two quick knocks, then Wohnt's voice. "Who's on duty?"

When I'd ducked, the library had been empty except for Mrs. Berns.

"Hello?" Wohnt's voice was impatient. I heard him step away from the desk and stride to the far wall, near the fiction paperbacks rack, before returning to the front, moving closer to the gate that would admit him behind the counter. My heart thudded sideways.

"Anyone?" he said.

From where I was shaking, I could see his hands curl round the swinging gate parallel to me and begin to push it open. Not only had he discovered my fingerprints on Chief Wenonga's post, but he was also about to find me hiding in a cupboard in the library. *Not good.* I tried to scrounge up a solid lie, but my brain had gone white.

I was going to jail.

"They don't teach you how to read in cop school? That there gate says 'Employees Only.'"

Mrs. Berns's voice stopped Wohnt in midopening. He released the gate. It creaked shut. Mrs. Berns brushed past him and stood on the other side of the gate, arms crossed, directly in my sight line.

Relief left me lightheaded.

"Where's Mira James?" Wohnt demanded.

"Probably chasing after that Johnny Leeson, if she's got any brains."

Jeez Louise. Did everyone know?

Wohnt's voice came out as a growl. "She's not working?"

"Nope. I've been promoted to vice president of the library, and today is my first day running the show. Can I help you find a book? Oh!" She pursed her lips and tilted her head dramatically. "That's right. You can't read."

Wohnt's fist dropped once, hard, on the countertop, and I heard him suck in a deep breath. When he spoke, his words came out slowly. "When you see Ms. James, tell her I need to speak with her. Immediately, if not sooner."

Mrs. Berns saluted. "Over and out."

I didn't move, even after I heard the front door open angrily and then swing shut.

Mrs. Berns kept her eyes forward. "Vice president," she mused. "That means I probably need a raise."

"Deal," I said weakly. "Thank you."

"You're welcome." She smiled down at me. "Say, did you hear Charles Manson is coming to town for the Fourth of July parade? I'm so excited!" With that, she returned to her reshelving, and I crawled out of the cupboard, still trembly, and took stock.

Not only did I need to locate a gigantic fiberglass statue and a semi-scalped man, but I also had to accomplish this while avoiding

Gary Wohnt and his posse. That's why I decided to sneak out of work during my lunch break, leaving the new vice president to handle the patrons and lock up.

Thankfully, no SWAT team awaited me at the double-wide, just Luna and Tiger Pop greeting me with love and warm indifference, respectively. I rushed inside to grab all three of us fresh food and water—kibbles for the dog and cat, an American cheese and sliced pickle sandwich on wheat for me. After our tummies were full, I took Luna for a walk and Tiger Pop for a follow down to the beach at the end of my driveway. Luna romped in the water, enjoying the coolness. While she swam, I scoured the woods for wild catnip for Tiger Pop and stumbled on a bumper crop. After Luna had gotten her fill of the lake, the three of us moseyed back to the house, where I did some dusting, vacuuming, and bathroom scrubbing. They cheered me on, silently, from a cool spot on the kitchen linoleum.

The whole time, I listened for the crunch of police tires purring down my gravel.

When suppertime neared, I tucked my hair beneath a baseball cap and changed into touristy clothing—a pair of white shorts I found in Sunny's storage room and a pastel-blue blouse I'd bought for my last job interview. Battle Lake was a small town, but it was overrun by strangers in the summer, particularly around the Fourth and Wenonga Days. If I rode Sunny's bike the three miles to town and wore my hat, I hoped to blend right in.

If I took the blacktop, I'd have a thigh-busting number of hills but some shade, and it was still as hot as orange stove rings outside. The gravel road, on the other hand, meandered through fields and so was flatter but also tree-free. I hopped on my bike, the muggy air licking at me like the devil's tongue, and opted for the route offering shade. My bike had only three gears, but I managed to make it all the way to town without needing to dismount and walk up any hills. I was proud, but sweaty.

Thankfully, Battle Lake was hopping. The Adirondack chairs out front of Granny's Pantry were crammed with pink-faced toddlers squalling in their parents' laps and sticky kids eating ice cream cones bigger than their heads. Down the street, Ace Hardware was featuring a Fourth of July weekend special, which meant that they'd stay open until nine. A row of shiny Weber grills lined the sidewalk to tantalize the tourists.

Farther up the street, Stub's Dinner Club, which looked like an enormous blue pole barn any way you sliced it, was packed to overflowing. Patrons were parking in the Larry's lot across the road to wait in line for one of Stub's famous butter knife steaks with a side of lyonnaise hash browns cooked by Lance Christianson, a locally famous chef.

Carefree summer chatter filled the air, and every third truck on the main drag pulled a boat. As I biked past the Dairy Queen, sniffing the smell of roasting burgers, I caught snatches of a lighthearted squabble over whether leeches or swamp frogs worked best for catching walleye. I kept my head down, confident that I was not conspicuous.

The Rusty Nail occupied a choice corner in downtown Battle Lake, and its log cabin exterior was welcoming. I was relieved that the place was packed so I could blend in. So far, I was batting whatever was a really good number to bat.

The Nail was plump with beer air and people out early in anticipation of the street dance, which would be held on the paved street right outside the Nail's front door. The band Kennie had booked for tonight was called Not with My Horse. She swore they covered country and rock favorites and would be real crowd-pleasers. I didn't listen to much country, and I wasn't looking forward to hearing "You Shook Me All Night Long" for the quadrillionth time, but the horde would provide great cover later as I sought out information on the missing Chief.

I located a table in the poorly lit poolroom and waited for Jed. I knew the police would be busy handling crowd control tonight, but I didn't want to take any chances, so I kept my back to the door.

"Mir? That you? What're you, in-cog-neeee-to?" Jed wore a dark-blue bandanna tied over his curly hair like a pirate helmet, a faded Rolling Stones T-shirt with a gigantic red tongue on the front, and Levi's, his hobbit-haired toes poking out of flip-flops.

I signaled for him to be quiet. "Shh! Sit down."

"What's up with you?" he said, sitting across from me. "You're acting all nervous and weird."

"It's this Chief Wenonga stuff," I said, glancing around surreptitiously. "You heard anything new?"

"The cops don't know nothin', and no one's seen the Chief." He whooped and slapped his knee. "Wohnt's pretty cheesed off. Makes him look like an idiot! He's running around town kickin' butt and taking names."

I dropped the menu I'd been holding. I didn't feel so hungry anymore. Jed continued, oblivious to my discomfort.

"I stayed and watched them scrape that piece of head off the post. I suppose they'll have some DNA soon enough, but I don't know what they're expecting to do with that." He scratched his head underneath the handkerchief. "They'd be better off looking for a guy with a hat!"

"What?"

"A guy with a hat." Jed smiled like I was the slow one. "Cuz he's missing a piece of his head?"

Suddenly, the Nail felt greasy and constricting. "That's a rich one, Jed. Um, I'm not feeling so good. Can I take a rain check on supper?"

Jed's face fell. "Sure. No problem. How about tomorrow, same time, same place?"

"I'll call you, 'kay?" I ducked outside with my head down and veered into the alley running behind the Nail to inhale some fresh air. Spindly elms grew around the dumpster, and I saw the logs on the front were just cheap siding. The rear was crumbling brick.

I ducked into a dark nook, upwind from the garbage, and collected my thoughts.

Wohnt was after me because my fingerprints had been discovered next to a bloody scalp. I had no alibi for last night, and my behavior had been suspicious pretty much since I'd moved to town. I was formulating a plan to clear my name when a voice cut through my schemes, addressing me directly.

"Now, this was the last place I expected to find you," it said.

Chapter 11

I squeaked and jumped back, scraping my elbow on the brick.

The melodic voice laughed. "Sorry, Mira. Didn't mean to scare you, but you *are* hiding in the alley behind a bar."

I rubbed the raw spot on my elbow and glared at Dr. Castle. Had she been following me? Her eyes were guileless, and she smiled warmly, her mouth as wide as the Cheshire cat's. I relaxed half a notch.

"I'm not hiding." I squinted up and down the alley to make sure no one else was sneaking up. A laughing couple in clicky cowboy boots strolled past a hundred yards away, but otherwise, the coast was clear. "I came out here to get away from the cigarette smoke. What're *you* doing in the alley?"

"Looking for you." She tipped her head, washing her eyes in shadow. "I stopped by early for a bite, and your friend told me you'd just left. If the smoke bothers you, we could go somewhere else."

The abrasion on my elbow made me crabby, and I wanted to just come out and ask if she'd stolen the Chief, but she didn't know me, and I didn't know her. "How about the Fortune Café? They have a deck off the rear."

"Perfect!" She was still in shadow. "I've been meaning to check out that place since I got to town. Mind if we walk?"

"Not at all."

If she wondered why I kept to the back streets, my head down, she didn't ask. When we reached the Fortune, I sent her to the deck to grab a table and pulled Sid aside. I explained that I was avoiding Wohnt, and though her eyes widened, she didn't ask questions. I brought out herbal iced teas and sugar cookies and sat down across from Dr. Castle.

For the first time, I noticed what a gorgeous night it was going to be. The sun had two hours left on the horizon, and it was reflecting pinks and dusty purples off the treetops, the intense heat making the colors more vivid than usual. The air smelled like lake water and grilling meat, and I could hear firecrackers popping and a family laughing in their backyard. The cheerful summer sounds would be drowned out in exactly one hour by the twang of raucous country guitars, but for the moment, Battle Lake was beautiful. I forced myself to relax. I needed Dr. Castle to feel comfortable enough to confide in me.

"How do you like Battle Lake so far?" I asked. I was actually a little intimidated by her now that we were one-on-one in a social setting. As recently as last winter, I'd been a professional college student, and although we were around the same age, she seemed more confident and loads smarter.

"You can call me Dolly," she said, squeezing her lemon into her tea, "and I like the town just fine. The people seem very warm."

"Really?" I didn't hide my surprise well.

"Really." She chuckled. "What, you thought they'd be mean to me because I'm taking away the Chief?"

"You mean, you *were* taking the Chief, until he disappeared."

"Funny timing, that." Her eyes grew hooded above her Cheshire mouth, and I couldn't tell if she was relaxed or hiding.

"Mm-hmm." I sipped my iced tea. The chill was delicious, but it was mostly flavorless. "So, since he's gone, your work here is done?"

"Oh no." She licked the lemon juice off her fingers, then stirred her tea with the straw. "Chief Wenonga was the symbol of the sort of thing PEAS is fighting, but he wasn't ever the only problem. I'm hoping to do away with the festival entirely."

I stirred sugar into my icy tea and played devil's advocate, hoping to mine some information. "Is the festival so bad? People don't even really know what they're celebrating. They just want an excuse to gather and have some fun."

It was a plausible argument. In Otter Tail County, where we outshone the country in per capita sales of fishing licenses, we had 1.004 men for every woman, the median age was 41.1, and the mean temperature was not much higher, people deserved distractions.

"Ignorance isn't an excuse, am I right?" The question came out gently, but I noticed her neck tense. "Objects sacred to the First Nations are being used as tourist attractions, and that's offensive. Stereotypical representations of Native American men, like the Chief Wenonga statue, limit the history of their ancestors to that of violent warriors. It also ignores modern cultural experiences of Native folks, not to mention overlooking Native women and children. It's destructive."

"Maybe we should be grateful Battle Lake didn't erect a drunken Irishman statue alongside the Chief," I said. "Though that might appease Les." I hoped my lame joke would get a reaction from her, but she sat still, studying me. I changed the subject. "You know they found fingerprints at the statue's base, right? It won't be long until they match those with the culprit."

Still no movement, aside from her mouth. "The *culprit* would need to have their fingerprints in the system, wouldn't they?"

I blinked once, then again. Of course! If a person had never been caught breaking the law, they wouldn't ever have been fingerprinted. If they'd never been fingerprinted, there'd be no way to match them to a crime unless they were already a suspect. I laughed with joy. As long as no one had witnessed me at Halverson Park this morning, or could trace the 911 call to me, I was safe. I just had to stay under Wohnt's radar until I tracked down the statue thief, who was possibly also a murderer.

I grinned at Dolly Castle, who appeared to be laughing silently at me. "You look like you just got a call from the governor." She arched an eyebrow and leaned forward. "Maybe you have something you want to confess?"

For a second, I considered that we could be friends, but not before I was permanently off the hook and someone else was on. And that someone might still turn out to be Dolly.

I backed off my smile. "How're the cookies?"

Dolly's glance, which she directed over my shoulder and at the door to the main café, grew steamy. "They just got considerably better."

I craned my neck, keeping the bill of my cap down, to see what had put the purr in her voice.

My gray eyes connected squarely with Johnny Leeson's deep blues.

Chapter 12

Somehow, in the few days since I'd last seen him, I'd forgotten how beautiful Johnny was, with his shaggy, dark-blond hair, thick eyelashes, and soft, gently smiling mouth. His hands were strong and tanned, the kind of hands that you wanted roaming slowly down your naked back and tangled in your hair as he pulled you in for a deep kiss.

His broad shoulders tapered nicely to narrow hips, and it took all my willpower not to imagine what it would be like to have my legs wrapped around them. I crossed said legs to muffle the excited whispering down below and gave him a short nod. Men'd always been bad news for me—in a cheating/dying sort of way—and I'd vowed to start listening to my brain more and my nerve endings less. It was high time I focused my energy on a more reliable form of entertainment. Like tornado chasing.

I had to suck in a deep breath and concentrate on slowing down my heartbeat, though, which had revved up at the sight of Johnny.

I wasn't surprised when Jed followed him out onto the Fortune deck. The two were the local odd jobbers, taking on landscaping and heavy lifting work on the side, and they often hung out after finishing a gig. I hoped Jed wouldn't feel bad to see that I was still out after ditching him. Johnny waved with one of his gorgeous hands before pulling up a chair at a far table, but Jed loped over.

"Hey, Mira!" he said, his voice loud even though he was only a few feet away and closing in. "You must be feeling better. And you know what I forgot to ask you? Now that someone stole the Chief, who you gonna crush on?" He slapped his knee.

Where was spontaneous combustion when you needed it? Clearly, my pitiful, make-believe love life was written on my forehead. Or more likely, a billboard on the edge of town. "Good one."

I tried to emanate powerful "go away" vibes. I didn't want Johnny to overhear that I thought Chief Wenonga was hot. If finding out that you crush on big fiberglass men doesn't turn a guy off you, then you don't want him.

Jed, as always, was oblivious to social cues. "You guys got extra chairs. Awesome!" He signaled to Johnny, who stood and strode over, flashing his killer shy smile as he made his way.

"Hey, Mira. How're you doing?"

I kept my head down. "Fine."

He indicated the two open chairs. "Mind if we sit here?"

"Not at all," Dolly murmured, sliding out the one nearest her. "I don't believe we've met."

I thought I detected a faint burning smell. It might have been the sizzling heat Dolly was directing at Johnny, or possibly my hopes of being the object of his unrequited love going up in smoke. I had no choice but to make the introductions. "This is Johnny Leeson. He works at the greenhouse here in town. And this is Jed." Jed smiled and nodded around a mouthful of our sugar cookies, but the professor didn't bother to glance his way.

"A horticulturalist? That's so fascinating! Where'd you study?" Dolly's smile was ear to ear, and she was leaning forward to hear Johnny's response.

He pulled back a hair, or maybe it was just wishful thinking on my part. "A state university." He looked over at me, and my pulse quickened. "I'm going to grab a couple sodas. Can I get you two anything?"

"Soda?" Dolly asked, touching his wrist lightly to bring his focus back to her. "The college must have been out of state. Everyone in Minnesota calls it 'pop.'"

"Yeah, it was U of W—plus my grandparents live in eastern Wisconsin. I spent a lot of summers at their place." He pointed at our sweating glasses of tea. "So you two are fine?"

"Yeah, we're fine. Thanks," I said. When Johnny stood up, I caught a whiff of him. He smelled clean and solid, like a cherry Popsicle stick. I forced myself not to ogle his beautifully sculpted rear as he walked away.

"Hey, you're the Indian doctor, aren't you?" Jed asked Dolly.

"Close." She finally acknowledged him. "I'm a professor of Native American Studies. What do you do?"

"Right on," he said, nodding. "I work at my parents' resort. It's a pretty good job, but . . . oh, dang!"

Before you could say "up in smoke," Jed leaped up from his chair and launched himself over the railing of the Fortune Café deck with surprising agility. I glanced over to see what had made him scurry and was alarmed to make out the bumper of a black-and-white pulling up in front of the café. I hoped the officers inside the vehicle hadn't been able to see who was seated out back, especially in the dusky light.

I was pretty sure that Gary Wohnt didn't have anything on me, but I didn't like the way he kept turning up. Maybe somebody *had* spotted me at Halverson Park after all. I glanced at Jed's retreating figure, then at the door Johnny had just left through. Would I rather risk going to jail, or leave Dolly alone to flirt with Johnny? Cripes. It was tough being single. I dropped two bucks on the table for a tip and jumped over the rail.

"I better go see what's up with Jed," I hollered. "Tell Johnny bye from me."

Dolly smiled but didn't respond. *Sigh.* Johnny was all hers.

I darted through back alleys, listening to the screech thump of the street dance band warming up, until I reached my bike parked away from the streetlights' glare near the Rusty Nail. I'd never intended to check up on Jed, who probably at this very moment was burying a roach and a packet of Zig-Zags in someone's backyard. I just needed to steer clear of the law. Since I was on the move, I might as well swing past the Meat and RV Store.

The back streets were starting to fill with cars as people arrived for the dance. I threaded around opening car doors and couples walking hand in hand, laughing at private jokes. The simmering air scraped over me as I pedaled, washing thoughts of Johnny out of my head.

For now.

Chapter 13

When I reached Meat and RV, I was happily surprised to discover a light still on inside. It was dim, filtering from the back room through the wide front window, but it gave me hope that Les was around. I leaned my bike against the building and crunched up to the main door. The CLOSED sign was face out, but I could see shadows playing against the back room's light.

I crept to the rear of the building just as the back door slammed open. I retreated into the shadows out of instinct and was only able to catch a sideways glimpse of the person leaving. It definitely wasn't Les. This guy was over six feet tall, with dark hair pulled back in a ponytail. His nose was sharp and arrogant, and his full lips were pressed tight in anger or concentration.

He strode toward a bloodred Hummer I hadn't noticed parked behind a Winnebago up on blocks. An image abruptly sewed itself into my mind—a picture of the red Hummer in my rearview mirror, tailgating me like a dingleberry. Not many of those beast vehicles around, even in the summer. Could this guy be the same person I'd seen driving toward Chief Wenonga's post this morning?

I'd take that bet.

I heard the *beep beep* of a security system unlocking the Hummer doors, which was a funny sound in Battle Lake. Most locals didn't secure their houses, let alone their cars.

Before Tall, Dark, and Angry escaped, Les flung himself out the back door. He wore a Cenex cap that was too big for his head and threatening to tip off. "Wait!"

The stranger hoisted himself into the vehicle. "I don't think so."

"But it's a good idea!" Les was running toward the Hummer, which rumbled awake and carried its mysterious passenger away before Les could reach it. He watched it go, delicately adjusting his hat.

"Les?"

He jumped. "Who's there?"

"It's me, Mira. From the library?" I stepped out of the shadows. "How're you?"

"Don't ask." Les kicked past me, a tight ball of resentment in his camouflage T-shirt and pants. He didn't glance my direction as he reentered his shop and slammed the back door. The lock clicked on the other side.

"Les? Mr. Pastner?" I knocked on the door. "I just want to ask you a couple questions about the Chief Wenonga statue. Mr. Pastner?" I kept drumming on the metal door for a minute or two before I gave up. If there was anything a militia guy was good at, it was waiting.

From the direction of town, I heard the muffled twang of an electric guitar ripping up a string of chords. The street dance was beginning. I could head to it and try to hook up with Dolly again, though staying out in public increased my risk of jail time. Possibly even worse, it would give Johnny more chances to see me in these deeply unattractive tourist clothes. The alternative, though, was going home to try and hide from Wohnt.

Put that way, my decision was easy.

Life had taught me that a moving target was harder to hit.

I walked my bike the five blocks back to the street dance, weaving around the latecomer cars scrabbling for a parking spot and pedestrians laughing and drinking beer out of plastic cups. The mood was festive. It was early enough that there were still kids out, thrumming with excitement to be among the grownups at night.

I couldn't squeeze my bike past the throng outside the Rusty Nail, so I walked it across to Larry's parking lot and hid it behind a row of yellow-blooming potentilla shrubs, careful to avoid the streetlights.

The closer I drew to the street dance, the more heinous the music became. Fortunately, pretty much any live tune would do if you were outside on a hot summer night with an icy beer and good friends, and the crowds I passed seemed to be either ignoring the music or laughing at it. I decided to walk the perimeter, where it'd be quieter. I didn't spot Dolly Castle or Johnny anywhere. I supposed they could still be on the deck at the Fortune, but I didn't have the heart to check.

As the crowd began to thin a few blocks up from the band, two flashing balls the size of apricots caught my attention. It took me a second to realize they were battery-lit earrings, and one more to see they were attached to Kennie. *Oh no.* I hurled myself behind an oak tree and peeked out. She stood about forty feet away. We were on the edge of the residential part of Battle Lake, right where the businesses ended and homes started. She was talking to the angry-pretty Hummer driver, and they were striding toward me. Their conversation drifted over the cat-song music.

". . . so embarrassed the Chief has gone missing."

"Don't worry, Kennie," he said, the streetlamps making right angles of his cheekbones. "It'll be fine."

She caressed his arm and giggled into his eyes. I was put off by her sloppy flirting. Even though she and Gary Wohnt went to great pains to hide their relationship, the whole town knew they were dating, and her current light infidelity was not a good look.

"I know it will, Brando," she said. "I'm absolutely certain."

Brando.

Mr. Hummer must be the owner of the company that created Chief Wenonga. He was walking like a man proud of himself, tall and strong, swinging his glossy black hair and cutting eyes at Kennie. It all begged the question: What had the owner of an out-of-town fiberglass company been doing at Les's Meat and RV?

Suddenly, the silence was deafening. The band was taking a break, and Kennie and Brando were almost on top of me. I slid around the tree inch by inch as they neared, staying just out of their view. I waited for a count of twenty, listening to their footfalls grow fainter. Then I scooted out to follow them, my eyes darting side to side, which was exactly why I didn't notice the solid, six-foot-two-inch mass in front of me until I railroaded right into it.

My eyes slowly traveled up the unyielding, muscular body to the face, my heart thudding. Had I misjudged? Had Brando backtracked to catch me?

When my reluctant eyes met the guy's gaze, my heart stopped and I froze solid as a glacier.

Oh, this was *much* worse than Brando.

Much worse than anything I could have dreamed up in my darkest nightmare, as a matter of fact.

Chapter 14

Bad Brad.

The man-shaped, turd-scented shoehorn who'd wedged me out of Minneapolis.

He and I'd been in an exclusive relationship, or so I'd believed. The last time I'd seen him, his eyeballs had been crammed shut in bliss while the woman dog-sitting for my neighbor played his skin flute. She'd been accompanied by the hard-to-find Portuguese woodwinds CD that I'd recently purchased for Brad. He didn't know that I'd caught them in flagrante delicto, as I'd been perched on the second-story roof of a West Bank apartment spying down from a skylight.

Shortly after I witnessed Mr. Cheater Pants in the act, he got into a mysterious bike accident. Seemed the nuts holding his front tire to the rest of his bike had disappeared. I felt bad, for a minute. Then I packed up and moved to Battle Lake, never telling him why we were through. It hadn't seemed particularly important that he knew. Or was it that I hated confrontations?

"Mira?" He grabbed my shoulder and held me an arm's length away, a look of happy surprise on his face. "Did you drive from the Cities to see my show?"

Brad was still cute, in his blond Jim Morrison sort of way. And still as dumb as a thumb. "Hi, Brad. No, I live here now."

He looked around, like he couldn't believe it. "In Battle Creek?"

"Battle Lake."

"Yeah. You hear us play? We're tight!" He brushed his hair back and stared at me with his clear brown eyes, smiling eagerly.

Had I really dated this doofus? He was seeing me for the first time since I'd disappeared and had *zero* curiosity about why I'd left or what I'd been up to since. "The street dance flyers said Not with My Horse is a country band," I said, confused. Brad exclusively played punk rock the last I'd heard.

"Oh, we are! But with our own style, you know?" He tapped his ear. "That last song? It was 'My Achy Breaky Heart Belongs to Satan.' Effin' cool shit."

I groaned. I'd let this man see me naked. I'd served him bacon and pancakes in bed. Heck, I'd even listened to his poetry and told him it was *luminous*. Running into exes was its own special brand of hell, wasn't it? Reminded you what a blockhead you used to be. Well, even monkeys could learn from their mistakes. "Hey, it was nice seeing you," I said. "But I gotta run." *Forever.* "You take care now."

"Not so fast!" He pointed toward the stage. "You should definitely stay for our next set. There's a song about you in there."

I'd been swiveling away, but that stopped me cold. "What?"

He mistook my horror for disbelief at my good fortune. "Yup," he said magnanimously, shining his fist on his chest.

I didn't want to ask but had to know. "What's it called?"

"Mira Mira."

Before I could react, Brad dropped to one knee and clutched my hand, belting out the tune in a wailing country twang: "Mira, Mira, on my wall, tell me who is the rockingest fool of all, no wait a minute, I think I see, the answer's staring back at me."

This was not helping me to blend in. I tried to reclaim my hand.

Brad stood, swiveling his hips and raising his voice, still clutching me tightly. Out of the corner of my mortified eyes, I spotted a crowd beginning to gather.

"Oooh! Mira, Mira on the wall, spent most of my life lying in bed, breakfast was vodka-soaked bread, and a pack of cigarettes." He was nearly yelling now. "Yow! Mira, Mira, then I met you, looking like Winona Ryder but hey you're a fighter, and they say you'll kill me, but I got a feeling, if I head next door for some loving, I'll start healing. Woo-ooo!"

Was he really singing about cheating on me, *to me*? I glanced around at the handful of people swaying to Brad's painful anti-serenade and wondered how long it'd take to chew off my hand so I could escape into the night. That's when I spotted Johnny and Dolly strolling toward us, her arm looped in his. My heart dropped from my chest into my stomach and then all the way to the ground, rolling around in the dirt.

Johnny and Dr. Dolly.

It was bad enough they were together, but I'd be damned if I'd let them see me being howled to by this mistake. I flicked Brad in the nose like the bad, bad dog he was. When he released me to rub his face, I sprinted toward my bike. I hopped onto it and pedaled furiously until I reached County Road 83, which I hung to for about half a mile before I turned onto the gravel, leaning into the hot, heavy air, letting it dry the tears on my cheeks. When I arrived home, I was too wired and depressed—no closer to finding the Chief, had lost Johnny to a better woman, and had a mortifying ex in town—to sleep.

No choice but to hit the garden.

It'd been a fertile year, with the unusually hot weather alternating with strong rains. My tangled backyard was as dense as a jungle, and the apple trees on the perimeter were thick with sour, baby-fist-size fruit. I changed out of the dorky tourist clothes into my uniform of faded cutoffs and a tank top, the night air still a moist eighty-two degrees according to the sun-shaped thermometer hanging outside my front door. I could smell the heavy sugar-scent of roses blooming, and below that was threaded the aroma of woodsmoke. Somebody must be having a bonfire. The smell of wood burning on a warm summer night spelled comfort for a Minnesota gal. It was in our genes. I resolved to force thoughts of Brad and Johnny out of my mind.

Back into the junk drawer for those two.

I gardened by moon- and yard-light, starting in on the east side of the bed with the row of marigolds. They were orange and spicy, their thick furry leaves casting too much shade to allow many weeds to take root below. That row was clean in under ten minutes. Next, I hoed the wide space between my staked tomato plants. These were flowering like mad, and before I weeded the base, I snipped the sucker leaves in the fork of the branches so the remaining plant would have more vigor to bear fruit. The snipped baby leaves left a wet, peppery streak on my fingers. Once the tomatoes were weeded, the earth around them as clean and warm as a brown blanket, I moved on to the onions, planting one foot on each side of the row as I gently dug out the pigweed sprouting between the bulbs.

Tiger Pop and Luna stretched themselves out on the grass at the edge of the garden and ignored me as best they could. By the time I finished the onions and swung over to the row of coffee can–clad broccoli, cauliflower, and brussels sprouts, the bugs were as solid as stew. Not for the first time, I wished mosquitoes had radiant butts like fireflies so they could at least light the way as they drilled into skin. If they had the power to glow, tonight'd be lit up like the northern lights.

Swatting at the buzzing horde, I dashed for the house, my hard-earned respite gone. Tomorrow was the Fourth of July, and I needed to evade the police in case they discovered I'd been first on the scene the day Chief Wenonga had disappeared, find a man missing part of his head, and track down a twenty-three-foot statue. While I was juggling that fun to-do list, I also needed to cover the fireworks display for the *Battle Lake Recall*, avoid a cheating ex-boyfriend who may or may not be spending the weekend in town, and convince myself that I hadn't really been falling for Johnny.

The only silver lining was that the library would be closed for the holiday, so I'd have time to nose around.

The first person on tomorrow's To-Snoop list was definitely shifty Les Pastner. He'd evaded me twice, first by not being at the Meat and RV this morning and second by locking the door on me tonight. I scratched at a mosquito bite behind my ear and thought about maybe wearing a hat next time I night weeded to deter the bugs from my more tender areas.

A realization dropped into place with such force that I gasped.

Les, who'd been acting awfully suspicious since the fake Wenonga Days planning meeting, had been wearing a hat, one perched oh so tenderly on his head, as he chased after Brando.

Click.

Of course.

Jed had joked that the police should look for a person wearing a hat because he'd be missing part of his scalp. Despite the heat, the image made me shiver.

If I couldn't force him to talk to me, at least I could peek under his cap.

Chapter 15

The Fourth of July dawned hot and bright.

The air was sticky, and out my front window the sun sparkled off the serene surface of Whiskey Lake. It was going to be another breeze-free scorcher.

I hopped into an ice-cold shower to cool off. When I stepped out, I wrapped my hair in a bun to get it off my neck and slipped into a cotton baby doll sundress that let the air flow freely on my back and legs. Before I poured fresh water for Luna and Tiger Pop, I packed their bowls with ice cubes. I even retrieved two oranges from the fridge's crisper drawer, sliced them in half, and nailed them to the birdhouse in the shade of the large oak tree in my yard so the orioles could chill a little.

Birds and I didn't get along, and since they had the aerial advantage, I went out of my way to be nice to them. As far as I was concerned, they were the avian equivalents of playground bullies. Likely, my bird aversion had something to do with misplaced guilt. When I was four and a half, my cousin Heather and I discovered a robin's nest in our climbing tree. There were three newly hatched babies inside, their featherless skin translucent. Heather warned me not to touch them because then their mom wouldn't come back. I pretended to listen, but deep inside, I felt that I was meant to take care of one of those robins. It would grow up believing I was its mom, and it would sing on my shoulder just like in a Disney movie.

We would be *tight*.

Later, when I was supposed to be napping, I sneaked back to the nest and snatched the weak little thing. I concealed it in the very back of my sock drawer, which was little used in the summer. Next, I pilfered a pound of raw hamburger from the freezer and set it next to the baby. My attention span being what it was, I quickly forgot both baby and burger until the smell became thick. I pulled the baby bird out of my drawer five days after I'd placed it in there, tiny eyes closed forever behind see-through lids. The hamburger was greenish and flirting with maggots. I tossed the burger in the woods and buried the bird in a shallow grave next to my Barbie doll whose head I'd accidentally popped off.

I may have been only four, but I knew I was the reason the baby bird had died. Since then, I assumed the birds recognized me for what I was—a nest robber—and I avoided them at all costs. I pretended it was because I didn't like them, but the truth was, they had every reason not to like *me*. I remained eternally on guard for the retributive poop missiles.

My special Fourth of July community ed class led by Johnny was scheduled for ten, with the Wenonga Days parade right on its heels at eleven, followed by some Les-hunting at noon. That plan allowed me enough time to tackle my laundry, compose a shopping list, and write a postcard to Sunny, whose double-wide I was house-sitting. As far as I knew, she was still on a fishing boat in Alaska with her mono-browed lover, Rodney, but she'd given me the address of the company's central office, so I had someplace to send mail to. I mulled over what to tell her about the current Wenonga situation. I didn't like to lie, at least to my friends, and I didn't want her to accuse me of keeping anything from her should all this have a bad ending, but I also didn't want to make her worry.

I needed to word it just so:

Hey, Sunshine! It's so frickin' hot in this hometown
of yours that my freckles have melted. Luna is doing

fine, though I think she might be getting a little pudgy—I'm going to start taking her on more walks. As Chief Wenonga Days approaches, I can't help but notice something is missing. Isn't this the first time in your life you haven't been at a Wenonga Days parade?

Big love!

—Mira

I was covered. I hoped by the time Sunny phoned, which she did every two weeks or so, this would all be solved, the Chief would be back in place, and I'd have only good news to report.

Postcard written, I washed, dried, folded, and put away two loads of clothes; realized that I didn't need anything from the grocery store besides bagels, cream cheese, and orange juice; and let the animals outside with their ice water placed in the shade. House in order, I slid gingerly into my dragon's mouth of a car. I tuned my radio to the rock station out of Fergus Falls, rolled down the windows, and drove as fast as the gravel would allow to move some air.

It wasn't until I passed a police car on the north side of Battle Lake, parked amid the traffic of the weekend flea market, that I remembered that driving my car wasn't a smart move. On a bike, I could blend in. In my brown hatchback, I was a fish in a barrel.

I hunched down, trying to tighten my ear skin so the anticipated police sirens wouldn't sound so shriekingly harsh as Wohnt chased me down. When the air stayed blessedly silent minus the nasal twang of CCR floating out of my radio, I dared a glance in my rearview mirror. The police car was empty, its occupant likely patrolling the mayhem of the flea market.

Four blocks ahead, another police rig was parked, and I could just make out Gary Wohnt standing near it, steering cars away from the marked-off parade route. It was too early in the day to be dumb twice, so I lurched a sharp right and puttered down a parallel street, parking the Toyota in the rear driveway of my friend Gina's house. A quick knock at her door told me she wasn't home, but when I tried her door-knob, it turned. I went inside, grabbed a red, white, and blue Minnesota Twins baseball cap off the rack next to the door, left a quick note, and headed toward the high school, where Johnny's gardening class was meeting.

In most parts of the United States, community education classes weren't held on national holidays. In Battle Lake, a local ladies' gardening club had started a petition to have Johnny's classes held every Saturday morning, come holidays, hell, or high water. Their reasoning was that he was providing an important service to the community and that many of his students were tourists, who were the thickest on the weekend holidays. Both points were true, if you agreed that looking dead sexy lecturing in front of a chalkboard was an important service and that the out-of-town friends and family of the ladies' gardening club counted as tourists.

Inside the classroom, I slid into the back row, next to two chirpy women in their early twenties. They both had golden hair, and the fluorescent lighting picked up their perfect honey highlights. Their skin was tawny, their breasts impossibly full yet perky, and I bet I couldn't have found an inch of cellulite on them even if I pinched them head to toe in a vise grip, one inch at a time. I'd attended enough of Johnny's classes to know that they were young groupies. Meanwhile, I felt like a swamp frog wearing a patriotic hat.

They scooched their chairs over slightly as I sat down and whispered between themselves, glancing at me.

I decided it wasn't their fault they were so beautiful. "Hey. I'm Mira."

They both studied me for a beat or two and decided I wasn't competition. "I'm Heaven," said the blondest, "and this is Brittany."

I nodded. I knew the type—fresh out of high school, sure of their place in the world but ultimately lacking confidence in anything other than their immaculate makeup and hairless bodies. If they didn't wise up in the near future, they'd be married and pregnant within two years. "You guys like to garden?"

This sent them into peals of laughter. Heaven caught her breath first. "Naw, chick. We don't come for the gardening."

That's when Johnny walked in, thick hair curling around his sun-browned face. He scanned the room, eyes gliding over the roomful of women, stopping tentatively when he spotted me, before walking to the front of the classroom. My dirt-grimed fingernails from last night's gardening suddenly seemed conspicuous, so I sat on my hands.

Ribbit.

"Hello, everyone," Johnny said in his deep, rich voice. "Thanks for coming. Today, we're going to talk about the second sowings of beets and lettuce—when to do it, what types of seeds to use, and where and how to plant them." He nodded, smiling at each of us. "I'm glad you're here, and I want you to know that in this class, there's no such thing as a dumb question."

Heaven raised her hand. "What do you consider a dumb question?"

I rolled my eyes under the bill of the Twins cap. *I'd be surprised if she was smart enough to turn left, yet here she is, pretty pretty pretty as can be.* I pinched myself immediately after the ugly thought formed. I knew better than to turn against my fellow ladies.

"Heaven, right?" Johnny asked. "Don't worry about it. Just ask any questions you have." He smiled encouragingly and turned to the chalkboard. His arm muscles, lean from outdoor work, rippled as he scrawled notes.

Heaven and Brittany sighed dreamily.

We all had three tight packages of Seeds of Change organic seeds on our desks—one Detroit Dark Red beet, its packet featuring a depiction of lusciously maroon beets as plump as a pirate's jewels; one Buttercrunch lettuce with a picture of a thick and tender head of greens on its front; and one Emerald Oak Looseleaf lettuce with bright-green leaves as delicate and whorled as a baby's ears gracing the packet. I shook the Buttercrunch packet, enjoying the grainy sound of the seeds falling over one another.

Despite my best intentions to remain crabby and distant, I became lost in Johnny's smooth delivery as he explained that it was probably best to sow beets every two weeks for the first two-thirds of the summer to keep up a regular supply. I was a sucker for earth-friendly guys, and by the end of class, I'd almost forgotten that he was no longer mine. When he stopped at the end to take questions, Brittany shot her hand into the air, wafting a fruity dose of CK One my way.

When she caught Johnny's attention, she tossed her golden hair over her shoulder and leaned forward, showing the world her front butt as it spilled out of her tank top.

"Do you prefer to garden with gloves, or without?" she asked.

The class listened anxiously, all eighteen women eager to learn what Johnny wore when he gardened.

He answered with his characteristic honesty, oblivious to the adulation he was garnering. "I like to feel the dirt on my hands, so I garden bare."

A soft groan swept through the room.

"Any other questions?" he asked.

"Do you give home gardening seminars? Like at someone's house?" This second question came from Heaven, who was tracing a finger around the edges of her pink-glossed lips.

"Sure." He crossed his arms, and his muscles popped out. "Why don't you stay after class, and I can give you more information."

Heaven and Brittany squirmed in their seats at the invite, and that was the end of class. I scooped up my seeds and bolted toward the door.

"Mira?" Johnny was walking toward me as the rest of the class gathered their belongings and broke off into cliques to say their *see ya laters*. "Can you hang on a second? I'd like to speak with you alone."

Johnny Leeson wanted to talk to me?

Alone?

Chapter 16

He gently held my upper arm and guided me toward the hall, heat pulses radiating from where his caramel skin brushed mine. I was too flustered to recall if he'd ever intentionally touched me before. I was acutely aware of my dirty nails, stupid hat, and galloping heartbeat. Certain that Johnny was going to ask me why in the hell an industrial jazz country rocker had serenaded me last night, I looked everywhere but into his face.

He was silent for a few seconds, then asked quietly, "Is something wrong?"

I shook my head and kept studying my sandals, my blue-painted toenails peeking out.

"You were really quiet in class today."

I sighed, resigned, and stared up into his disarming, cobalt-blue eyes, trying to keep my voice light. "I've got a lot going on."

Just then, Heaven walked into the hall. "Can we talk, Johnny?"

"Sure," he said, waving her back into the classroom. "Give me a second." He touched me still. His hand felt warm and strong.

When Heaven was out of earshot, he turned back to me. "I want to talk to you, but the conversation might take a minute. Are you free tonight?"

My heart seriously skipped a beat. Was he asking me out on a date? All thoughts of Dolly and self-pity melted away and, with them, my newfound distant-cool attitude around Johnny. "I really like you!"

Johnny shot me a puzzled look, the corner of his mouth twitching. "You really like me?"

Sweet baby Jesus, I was going to have to join the circus and never come back. "No. I mean, I meant to say that I'd really like *to* . . . um, to do something with you later. If I'm free, you know, but I think I am." I guess a gal never got too old to be stupid *and* easy.

My sudden wave of uncool still had Johnny thrown. He dropped his hand from my arm. "Good. Yeah, good. I'll pick you up at six, and we can go out for supper."

I intended to say something that would linger with him until tonight. What came out instead was "I love supper!"

Johnny smiled a strange smile and walked back into the classroom.

I swallowed the doofy grin still planted on my face. Maybe I'd misjudged Johnny and Dolly's hanging out last night. They could have been talking about Wisconsin, for all I knew, since both had spent a lot of time there. I literally skipped to the front door and floated to the *Recall* office to pick up the digital camera before heading to the Kiddie Karnival.

The carnival was being held right off Lake Street in the fire hall's parking lot. It was actually a pretty lame event, if you knew better. If you were aged two to five, though, the fishing for plastic ducks, throwing darts at balloons, and tossing rings on old glass Coke bottles was nirvana, and everyone left a winner with a pocketful of Tootsie Rolls.

The turtle races—a Battle Lake summer staple no matter the week—were a little grimmer. The pavement at the First National Bank parking lot had been sprayed with hoses, but it seemed to be steaming slightly. I was worried the turtles were going to melt their little mitts right into the tar. The reptiles started in the center of the pavement, inside the permanently painted four-foot-diameter circle. The first turtle to make it outside the circle won.

Fortunately, there was a plastic wading pool filled with water and chilling turtles on each side of the track. Kids could choose a favorite filthy creature from the free-for-all pools or bring their own. It was a zoo, literally and figuratively. Much shrieking and turtle prodding ensued, and twenty minutes later, I was snapping pictures of the winner, Ashley Grosbain, holding her urinating reptile close to her face and grinning.

It was sweet.

Also, good birth control.

I left to hit Lake Street, where hundreds of people milled around in anticipation of the parade, some hauling treasures from the flea market, others licking sloppy cones, still others clutching popcorn from the Big Bopper. The Big Bopper had been driving his popcorn cart into town every July for as long as people could remember. I didn't know how he made ends meet. He sold caramel corn, kettle corn, regular popcorn, popcorn balls . . . if it had popcorn in it, the Bopper sold it, but never for more than fifty cents a bag. I didn't need to be a math whiz to figure out he'd need to sell a lot of popcorn to even cover his gas money. Not for the first time, I wondered if he was a wealthy eccentric who netted secret joy out of infusing the population with delicious fiber.

The Big Bopper knew me from previous summers, when I'd visited Battle Lake to see Sunny, and he never forgot a name. As I walked past his cart, he called out to me, "It's gonna be a busy weekend, Ms. James. Popcorn?"

I declined, but then thought better of it. It was never too early for kettle corn. I even bought two sapphire-blue, sugar-soaked popcorn balls to feed to the birds back at my place. It might keep them appeased for another day.

I found a good parade-viewing spot directly in front of Ace Hardware and settled myself on the curb between two families just as I heard the cacophonous sound of the high school band break into the opening bars of "Louie, Louie" on the north side of town. The Battle Lake Bulldogs inched their way through the crowd in hitches and spurts, stopping and starting as directed by their bandleader. By the time they reached me, they'd segued to "Apache" and then "Wipe Out," and were back to "Louie, Louie" again.

Behind the Bulldogs rode the Kiwanis, who hurtled by on their tiny little motorcycles, performing death-defying crazy eights while barely avoiding spectators and each other. They always got my blood racing. A string of convertibles and antique cars followed, the whole scene one of friendly, celebratory chaos. Then suddenly, a murmuring passed down the crowd, and I could see people standing up near the parade's headwaters. This movement rolled through the spectators like a wave, until I, too, was forced to my feet to see what was going on.

I groaned when I saw what had everyone whispering. Bringing up the rear of a 1953 navy-blue Chevy were two men, each holding the end of a pole on which hung a DIVERSITY IN BATTLE LAKE sign. This could only be Kennie's work, a knee-jerk response to Dolly's request for more cultural awareness.

Leading the "diverse" group were three white-skinned men wearing leather Indian outfits straight from a Hollywood wardrobe department, circa 1950. They actually looked like miniature, pale Chief Wenongas without the strength and beauty, and it made me sad. One of them held a sign that said, WE SUPPORT NATIVE AMERICANS, but they were beating their chests like Tarzan and whooping and hollering. The crowd near me clapped politely. In this area, folks were proud of their hyperliteral rendition of the Chief in the same way they rooted for global warming in the frigid winter—quietly, with a good dose of self-flagellation for being so selfish.

Mrs. Berns and her friend Ida followed closely in a golf cart draped with a LOVE AN OLD LADY banner. Ida looked as crisp as a fall apple, even in this unbearable heat. She wore a white sun visor with a matching tennis dress and shoes, not a curl out of place. Mrs. Berns was a little less conservative in her NASCAR tank top and bike shorts, but the outfit seemed appropriate, given the speed with which she was driving the cart.

At the end of the diversity exhibit came four Klitzkes, a family notorious for its farm machinery accidents. All four were dressed in street clothes. One held a sign that said, IMAGINE NOT BEING ABLE

TO PLAY VIDEO GAMES. The second had a sign that said, WHAT IF YOU COULDN'T HITCHHIKE? The third's sign read, ENVISION A LIFE WHERE YOU CAN'T SHOW APPROVAL TO SOMEONE STANDING FAR AWAY. The fourth and final member of the troupe brought it full circle with their sign: SUPPORT THOSE WITHOUT THUMBS (TWT).

The entire group chanted, "Support TWT," as they walked past, and sure enough, each of them was missing at least one thumb.

And that was diversity in Battle Lake.

Before I could wrap my head around it, the Battle Lake fire truck rolled past, its occupants beaning the crowd with purple taffy and drawing children from their parents like lemmings toward a cliff, scrambling for pavement-warmed candy. Next came more old cars, four really big horses looking lathered in the heat, glittering farm implements and an old tractor, and then what appeared to be a cheerleading group.

As they drew closer, I realized it wasn't just *any* cheerleading group. Kennie Rogers was at the head, wearing her patriotic cancan dress and red, white, and blue stovepipe hat from yesterday's crime scene. She was accompanied by twelve other women dressed identically, the youngest around fifty, and they were all chanting, "We got spirit, yes we do! We got spirit, how 'bout you? Goooo, Beaver Pelts!"

Between cheers, the baker's dozen of women handed out business cards. Kennie ran to me and stuffed one in my hand, her cheeks rosy with excitement. "Guess now you know what I've been up to. Cheerleading camp! It's called radical cheerleading, and it's the newest way to activate crowds and advertise products in the summer, what with all the parades across the state. You could be a Beaver Pelt, too!"

I pulled my hand away as if burned, but I couldn't keep from peeking at the raised brown letters against the card's white background.

RADICAL CHEERLEADERS FOR RENT
CONTACT KENNIE ROGERS AT BEAVERPELTS@PRTEL.COM
FOR MORE INFORMATION.

I glanced up just in time to witness Kennie and her group execute a painfully provocative choreographed hip-grind to Kennie's shouted cheers of "Don't hate us 'cause we're sexy! Don't hate us 'cause we're hot!"

Kennie was renowned for her odd business endeavors. In May, she'd tried hosting a geriatric party house before moving her attention to elderly beauty contests. I supposed the radical cheerleading shouldn't have been a surprise, but I was having a hard time digesting it.

Before I had a chance to really try, a red Hummer roared up on the tails of the Beaver Pelts. Brando pulled the mammoth vehicle to a halt, put it in park, and climbed half-out through the SUV's sunroof, megaphone in hand. Kennie rushed from the front of her Pelts to be nearer to his vehicle, all the while leading her group in a creakily seductive version of Pat Benatar's "Hell Is for Children" music video.

In the light of day, Brando was even more handsome than my first impression of him last night. His black hair, now loose and straight around his shoulders, accented his sharp cheekbones and straight nose, and his smooth smile was dazzlingly white. Apparently, I wasn't the only one who noticed his good looks, as the men around me began grumbling and the women's faces went slack. I wasn't impressed with him, though, if for no other reason than his obnoxious vehicle.

Never trust a man who pays for a Hummer.

"Ladies and gentlemen!" he said into the megaphone, the crackling loud noise making at least one sweaty infant start squalling. "Hello and thank you for inviting me to your beautiful town!"

I snapped some shots with the digital, then angled my head to watch him work the crowd. He was good. He appeared to make visual contact with every woman within distance. His erection eyes slid off one eager face to the next, leading me to wonder if he was going to whip out his flute and lead all the women of Battle Lake away like the pied piper.

"My name is Brando Erikkson, and my father created the Chief Wenonga statue for your town. Now, it's my understanding that the Chief has disappeared." At his mention of the missing statue, Brando hung his head, as if saddened. He waited one beat, two beats, three, then lifted his face, blinding the crowd with his grin. "But I have good news! Fibertastic Enterprises is going to donate a slightly irregular woodchuck to grace your beautiful town until the Chief is returned!"

Kennie squealed and applauded, and soon, the whole crowd was cheering good-naturedly. Brando clasped his hands in the air as if signaling a victory.

A *woodchuck?* That was *slightly irregular?*

I was distracted from the rest of Brando's speech as the golf cart that had carried Ida and Mrs. Berns came roaring back against the grain of the parade. Mrs. Berns was no longer in the cart, and an addled-looking Ida was yelling, "Someone stole the Indian! The Indian is gone!"

She was largely ignored as everyone stared, rapt, at Brando perched in his Hummer. The woman next to me muttered, "The old coot just figured out someone stole Chief Wenonga?"

I glared at the woman and rushed toward Ida, worried she was suffering from heatstroke. She was traveling an erratic pattern through the crowd. I lurched after her and almost had her steering wheel when she squirted away the other direction. I had to throw myself onto the back and crawl over the seat, pulling her foot off the pedal. "Are you OK, Ida?"

She stared at me, her eyes blazing. "Someone stole the Indian!"

"Shh, shh, Ida. It's OK." We were stopped at the side of the parade route. I patted her hand and looked around for water. "The police are searching for Chief Wenonga. It'll be OK."

Brando was still courting the crowd through his megaphone, but I couldn't pay attention to the words. I was about to holler for an ambulance when the panic in Ida's voice sliced through the thick summer air and forced me to look back at her.

"It's not the Wenonga statue," she said, her mouth trembling. "It was Randy Myers, one of the Indian impersonators from the parade. He's been kidnapped!"

Chapter 17

My ears began buzzing. "What do you mean, 'kidnapped'?"

"I mean, he was there, talking to me and Mrs. Berns, and then he was gone," she said, waving her hands in agitation. "The other two Indians don't know where he went. He's been taken by ghosts!"

My heartbeat calmed. This was *not* an emergency. "I'm sure there's a rational explanation. He probably just popped into the Rusty Nail for a beer."

Ida set her shoulders stubbornly. "Kennie wanted the parade to begin and end with Indians. He was supposed to walk back to the starting point so he could go through again, but he's disappeared."

Sure enough, as Brando dropped back into his Hummer, his speech apparently over, and the Beaver Pelts faced front again, I noticed two confused-looking guys in Indian costumes straggling from the rear. They were scanning the crowd and shrugging.

Still. "I'm sure it's fine, Ida. Why don't you go tell Gary Wohnt what's going on? I bet he'll find Mr. Myers real soon."

She appeared doubtful, but after I slipped out of the cart, she drove off toward the police station. I bought a bottle of icy water from a shiny-faced kid with a cooler before speed walking through the sticky crowd to the Meat and RV Store. I didn't know if Les was capable of kidnapping a statue *and* a man, but if he'd taken Randy Myers, he wouldn't have gotten far.

I cruised to the back of the shop, out of breath and miserable from the heat. Before I checked for Les, I pressed the chilled bottle of water against my face, trickled a little down my spine, and then chugged it all. I tossed the empty bottle into a nearby recycling bin and yanked on the back door. I don't know why I was shocked when it opened smoothly. I walked in without pausing, washed in the smell of smoked meat and car oil.

The back room appeared exactly like I had expected—open pizza boxes falling over piles of newspaper, gray file cabinets half-open, overflowing ashtrays heaped in corners. The place was a fire hazard and far too messy to snoop in. A computer printout on the top of a mound of newspapers caught my eye only because of its whiteness amid the dinge. "University of Wisconsin" was printed across the top. On closer inspection, I was shocked to see it was a printout of Dr. Dolly Castle's web page. It featured a photo of her smiling sedately alongside a list of the Native American Indian classes she'd be teaching in the fall, with links to syllabi. At the bottom was her contact information.

The next page was a printout from another website with a laminated card paper-clipped to it. The website was called the Man's Militia, and page one listed a statement of grievances against the United States federal government. The next page listed adversaries of the militia, but it was all general references to corrupt bureaucrats, law enforcement agencies, judges, and prosecutors.

The laminated card attached showed a grainy photo of Les Pastner, his full name—Lester Luther Pastner—his vital statistics, and a picture of a red flag featuring a blue x dotted with eleven white stars over the words "The Independent States of America." Les was taking this militia business seriously. I glanced around for a computer but didn't see one.

I strode to the front before I lost my adrenaline boner. This was the part of the store the customers saw, and it smelled cool and peppery. There was one refrigerated display case about the size of a couch next to the cash register, and it was packed with shrink-wrapped venison sausages and jerky. In the far corner, an old-fashioned metal desk was stacked neatly with Winnebago brochures. The corkboard to the left of the front door was plastered with notices for auctions, garage sales, and free kittens.

Other than the furniture, the room was empty, which left only one place to explore. Behind the till was a closed door made of the cheap wood found in prefabricated homes. I walked toward it, cockiness melting out of my step. I was trespassing in the workspace of a likely unstable militiaman who'd begun to wear a hat about the same time a piece of scalp had shown up at the Chief's empty statue base.

I forced myself forward, leaving a trail of cooling nerve behind me. One step, two steps, three steps, and the warm metal of the doorknob was in my hand. One turn, push, and I was inside the windowless room.

My eyes adjusted in seconds, and I moved forward into what could be generously described as a living space. There was an aging TV against one wall, its antennae covered in twisted aluminum foil. Next to the television was an open door that looked in on a toilet and sink. On the far wall of the room stood two folding chairs and a card table with a short leg. The next wall over was consumed by a couch.

Someone was sprawled on it.

I stepped back involuntarily, an image of Jeff's corpse in the library slapping me across both cheeks.

It didn't help that this body was laid out exactly like Jeff's had been, legs straight, arms crossed over his chest, with a hat instead of a book covering his face. I forced myself forward, my joints creaking stiffly. I reached down and toward the hat, the smell of hickory-smoked meat overwhelming my senses. I noticed distantly that it was a Cenex cap.

I felt as if I were swimming through Vaseline, my heart jittering in my chest. My fingers grasped the smooth cloth.

I lifted the hat gently away.

And then I screamed.

Chapter 18

Les Pastner was under the hat, and he slept with his eyes open.

He looked like a lizard-man.

How did his peepers not dry out? My scream startled him awake, and he leaped off the couch, pulling a shotgun from the crease between the back and seat cushions in one swift motion.

"I am ready. What in the hell, *I am ready!*" he yelled.

I jumped back and threw my hands over my head. "It's me, Les! Mira! From the library. Put down the gun."

Les kept his head on a swivel, searching for enemies in the corners. When he found only me, he lowered the gun and scratched his head. It was then I noticed he'd been the recipient of a really bad haircut that left him with patchy bald spots. His scalp was otherwise completely intact.

"Whaddya want, Mira?"

I lowered my hands. "I just have a couple questions, Mr. Pastner. For the paper. Do you have a minute?" Having a gun pointed at me made me feel like throwing up, but I needed to take advantage of the situation. I dropped my shaking body into one of the folding chairs, realizing I had no idea what to ask him.

"Jeezus. You scared me near half to death." He scratched at his head, his close-set eyes still pinging erratically around the room. At this distance, he reminded me a little of Mickey Rooney.

"Yeah, likewise," I said.

"You should know better than to sneak up on a man like that." He scowled. "It's probably best you go."

"Just a couple questions, please." I thought quickly. "What was Brando Erikkson doing here last night?"

Les ran his fingers over the peaks and valleys of his haircut and reached down for his hat. "We was working out a business deal."

"About what?"

He shoved his cap onto his head. "About none of your business."

My legs had stopped shaking. I could stand if I needed to. "Are you bothered that Chief Wenonga is gone?"

Les made a shooing motion. "I already talked to the police about Wenonga. I sell Meat and RVs, not statues. Got no use for 'em."

I had no choice but to stand, but I took my own sweet time meandering toward the door. "Did you know that another Indian disappeared today, this one a real human from the parade?"

That gave Les pause. "When was that?"

"Not a half an hour ago."

"Well, you saw me here, asleep. Right?"

I shrugged. "Just now, yeah, but I don't know what you were doing half an hour ago."

Les stopped herding me out and reappraised me. "Well, maybe we can make a deal. Maybe I can tell you something about Chief Wenonga gone missing, and you can remember you've been here for thirty minutes."

I turned, crossing my fingers behind my back, where he couldn't see. "Sure. You start. What've you got on Wenonga?"

"I know Dr. Dolly Castle been in town for two days, and if what you say about the parade today is true, two Indians have gone missing in that time." He tapped his head like he'd just shared something smart. "That's the tree you should be barking up."

My eyebrows furrowed. "Are you saying Dolly knows where Chief Wenonga is?"

He pushed up the bill of his cap. "I'm saying you should keep your eye on her."

That was a pretty lame quid pro quo, but since I had no intention of lying for Les, I supposed it was a fair exchange. He apparently thought we were done because he was shooing me out again.

"You know where Brando is staying?" I asked on the way.

"A cabin right north of town." Up this close, Les smelled lonely, like the inside of a pumpkin.

"What about Dr. Dolly Castle?" I persisted. "Where's she staying?"

"She's out at the motel."

Now I was completely outside, the bright sunlight all but melting my skin. "So you didn't take the Chief?"

Les Pastner looked me squarely in the eye. "I have no idea where Chief Wenonga is."

I had enough experience with the gray side of the truth to know I'd just been blown off with a non-lie, but before I could follow up, Les slammed the door in my face and slid the lock loudly into place.

It was then that I heard the sirens keening toward me. I was exposed, the nearest cover a fleet of rusty Winnebagos forty feet away. I opted for false bravado and strolled toward town, the bill of my borrowed Twins cap tugged low.

As the sirens approached, my strides grew longer. I could almost see the navy blue of the squad cars by the time the RVs were ten feet away, and I couldn't keep my cool any longer. I squealed like a boy and dived under an ancient GMC Jimmy Mini motorhome, scraping both knees, just as an Otter Tail County sheriff's vehicle tore into town, ripping toward the parade.

I hoped Randy Myers's corpse hadn't just been discovered.

Chapter 19

I dusted myself off and made my way back toward town, the gravel-studded skin over my knees pulling painfully with each step. The initial folks I encountered were throngs of happy tourists carrying Larry's Grocery bags weighted down with cheap parade candy. Gina was the first person I recognized, her familiar white-blonde hair shining in the sun, as she huffed toward Granny's Pantry.

Gina and Sunny had been good friends before Sunny split for Alaska, and I'd picked up where Sunny had left off. Gina was a skilled nurse with the heart of a randy saint. Her husband, Leif, was a philanderer, but he'd stayed true ever since I'd innocently happened upon some damning photos snapped of him covered in pro-PETA signs when he'd had one too many.

"Mira? Is that you under there?" Gina pulled off my Twins hat and grinned, her smile brightening her face. "You look like a dork. What in the hell are you doing in that stupid cap?"

"It's yours, *dork*." I grabbed the hat back and shoved it on my head. "No time to talk. Do you know why the county sheriff just zipped into town?"

"You haven't heard?" Her face grew worried. "There's been a kidnapping. Someone grabbed Randy Myers from the parade. I tell you, it doesn't pay to be an Indian in Battle Lake right about now."

"At least not a fake one." I glanced around, relieved, at least, that they hadn't found his body. "They're sure he isn't just out tying one on somewhere?"

Gina dug into her purse and came out with a packet of Laffy Taffy. She wasn't afraid to talk with her mouth full. "Pretty sure. He's a reliable guy, and he's disappeared. The cops are a little jumpy in the best of times, but two missing guys in two days isn't good, even if one is a statue."

I nodded. "You got any other dirt?"

Gina raised her eyebrows suggestively. "You mean like the kind Johnny Leeson was throwing around at his community ed class today?"

For a second, I let myself go there, to a world where Johnny and I gardened together. A picture of his lean upper body bending over a hotbed of sprouts blissfully decorated the corners of my mind. His hair would fall into his eyes, and I'd lean over to push it away. He'd smile, stop my hand halfway to his face, and tell me that he could no longer bear his life without spending some quality time in my loins. I'd demur long enough for him to throw me over his shoulder and carry me out to the garden patch for a little irrigating . . .

"Mira? I was kidding about Johnny." She snapped her fingers in front of my face. "Mira?"

I focused guiltily back on Gina, who'd moved on to Tootsie Rolls. Had I been drooling? I decided not to tell her about my pending meeting with him tonight. I didn't want to jinx it. "Of course you were. *Duh.* I was just thinking about how weird this town's been."

"You mean lately?" she asked. "Or since the mid-1800s?"

"Ha ha."

She smiled good-naturedly. "You want to go to the fireworks with Leif and me tonight?"

I'd forgotten about the fireworks. They might be a good opportunity to dig up more information, as long as it didn't interfere with my Johnny time. "Maybe. When're you going?"

"We're meeting some people for drinks at Stub's at eight and heading to Glendalough at nine thirty or so. The fireworks are supposed to start at ten."

"How 'bout I just look for you at Glendalough, by the pay stand, around nine forty-five?" Glendalough was a gorgeous state park north of town. It consisted of nearly two thousand acres of pristine prairie lands and six lakes that added another thousand acres, donated to the Nature Conservancy by the Cowles family on Earth Day 1990 and then passed over to the Minnesota Department of Natural Resources two years later. It was a favorite location for Fourth of July fireworks viewing, which were traditionally launched from the shores of Molly Stark Lake within its borders.

"Deal. Bring a blanket and mosquito repellent. And I've got some big news."

Probably she was getting her ears double pierced, or something on that scale. She liked to feign drama. She gave me a quick hug and headed in the direction of home, and I took off for the library. I moaned with ecstasy when I stepped inside, the air-conditioning a blessing on my burning skin. Some hair had escaped from my bun and lay like hot snakes against my neck. I tied it back up before heading to the bathroom to wash my raw palms and knees.

Once I was clean and cool, I pulled up my article in progress. I didn't have much to add to the original, except a new closing paragraph:

> In a surprising turn of events, Battle Lake resident Randolph Myers has disappeared from the Fourth of July parade. At the time of his capture, Myers was dressed as a Native American, his clothing comparable to the Chief Wenonga statue. The similarities between the cases have police baffled. Maybe these males are asking for it by the way they dress? Regardless, the police are currently investigating the missing statue and Myers and hope to have both returned safely.

While I was online, I searched for information on Fibertastic Enterprises. The first hit showed a one-page website featuring various fiberglass statues, chief among them my Wenonga. According to the site, Fibertastic Enterprises was located in Stevens Point, Wisconsin, a town about three hours southeast of Saint Paul. The page included a phone number and email address, both of which I jotted down.

I shut off the computer, locked up the library, and headed upstream against the parade lingerers, intent on uncovering more about Dolly. When I reached the twelve-room, log-sided Battle Lake Motel, it was apparent there was no red Hummer around, though there was no reason there should have been other than a nagging hunch I had that Dolly and Brando knew each other. I wasn't sure what kind of car Dolly drove, but the only vehicle in the lot with Wisconsin license plates was a black Honda Civic plastered in bumper stickers like KEEP YOUR LAWS OFF MY BODY, VIRGINIA IS FOR LOVERS, INDIANS DISCOVERED AMERICA, and THE FIRST BOAT PEOPLE WERE WHITE. I peeked in the car windows. Coca-Cola cans littered the floorboards, and a stack of CDs spilled onto the front seat.

Must be Dolly's.

I entered the motel's front office and pretended to admire the prints of ducks and dogs in the waiting space while the young woman working the front desk spoke on the phone. When she was free, I asked her if she knew what room Dolores Castle was staying in.

She smiled kindly. "I'm afraid I can't give out personal information about our guests, but I'd be happy to give Miss Castle a message for you."

"Can you tell me if that's her Honda Civic out front?"

Her smile faltered. "I'm afraid that's against motel policy. Sorry."

I scanned my brain for ways to trick her out of the information but came up blank. I figured my best bet was to wait on the fringes of the Halverson flea market next to the motel until either Brando or Dolly appeared or it was time to get ready for my Johnny rendezvous. I thanked the desk clerk and headed back into the early-afternoon heat.

I sidled up to the nearest flea market table, which, near as I could tell, sold the contents of various junk drawers from across the ages—rusty doorknobs, cheap Marlboro lighters, assorted tintype photos, pocketknives. All the stuff that you didn't want even when you owned it. I pretended to dig through the crusty treasures as I counted the minutes. The white-haired man running the booth gave up trying to sell me something about 3:00 p.m. At 3:30, I'd visited every table at the market. I was turning to go home when I caught a glimpse of a strawberry blonde walking down the motel walkway toward a room.

I tried to stroll away unobtrusively, furtively sniffing at the metallic smell of my fingers, stained orange from digging in junk. I'd need to wash these puppies. I ducked down as the reddish-blonde head turned toward me. Through the windows of the sedan I was hiding behind, I confirmed it was Dolly. She appeared flushed and happy. She popped in and out of her room, a golden 7 on its door, in under three minutes. She hurried to the black Civic and peeled out of the parking lot before I could say hi.

I walked casually to her door. A quick twist of the knob told me it'd locked automatically behind her, and the window shades were closed tightly. Where had she been off to in such a hurry, and what had made her so happy?

I started back toward my car, still parked at Gina's, when I had a flash of fear. Should I stop by the drugstore to prepare myself for my get-together with Johnny? It probably wasn't an official date, and even if it was, we likely weren't going to fool around, but what if we did and I was unprepared? I decided I had nothing to lose from a quick trip to the apothecary. If nothing else, it wouldn't be the first pack of condoms to expire, lonely and unused, in my bedside stand.

There was only one problem with this plan. Buying condoms was never fun, but in a small town where everyone knew your business, it could be horrifying. As an example of the small-town gossip train, last month, I'd ordered a caffeine-free Coke instead of my usual Coke

Classic with my lunch at the Turtle Stew. Three hours later, Gina phoned me at the library to ask if I was pregnant.

Things like that were why I was always careful to keep my business private as much as possible. There was no way around the condom issue, though, so I strode purposefully into the apothecary and straight to the embarrassing-stuff aisle.

There was a huge variety, but I'd long ago decided choosing which condom to buy was like picking which dish to order at a Chi-Chi's "Mexican" restaurant—they might have different names on the packages, but they were all the same inside. I grabbed the box nearest me and headed toward the counter.

Where I nearly barreled into Johnny, who was buying some sort of medication and a bag of balloons, his back to me.

I squeaked involuntarily and slapped my hand over my mouth, the other one holding a box of mortifying presumptions. Thank all that was good, he was so intent on paying for his items that he hadn't heard me. I carefully backed away until I was behind the endcap suntan lotion display, where I dropped the condoms like a bundle of itchweed. I grabbed the nearest magazine off the rack and walked back around to the counter.

"Hi, Johnny," I said, feigning casual.

He turned quickly, then moved to shield his purchases while the cashier bagged them. "Hey, Mira." He looked embarrassed, and as soon as the cashier handed him his sack, he hurried toward the door. "See you tonight!"

I shook my head. Was even Johnny going weird on me? I glanced absently at the magazine I'd grabbed, noting it was *Cosmo*, whose ads turned me off. I'd long ago decided I would rather be strong than skinny. I was about to return the mag when the splashy line on the cover caught my eye: "First Date Fears? Make Yourself Sweet and Sassy so He'll Love You Forever." Was it a sign, an arrow piercing a red heart, pointing from Johnny to me? I paid for the magazine, stashing it under my arm so no one would see me with it.

Once home, some quality pet time was my first order of business. I walked Luna the half mile to the mailbox and back, reminding her every few feet that she was a good dog. She needed that constant reinforcement. Tiger Pop, on the other hand, followed discreetly behind, sticking to the shade and just coincidentally sauntering in the same direction. Back at the double-wide, I scratched them both behind their ears and refilled their water bowls, again adding ice. Then I hopped into the shower to cool off. The clear and cool water felt great cutting through the dirty sweat coating me.

I dried off and bandaged my knees, clean but sore from the RV dive, and made myself a light snack of gouda and apples. I pulled out the *Cosmo* to read while my hair dried. The "First Date Fears?" article was on page 217, sandwiched between an ad for designer perfume and another for diamonds. I was not their target audience.

> OK, you've been chasing Mr. Dreamboat for weeks, and you've finally caught him! Now what do you do? Make yourself sweet and sassy, of course! Don't waste your time or his by showing up to this date less than fantabulous. Follow these five easy steps to make the night magically memorable. And who knows? It just might lead to marriage:

- Rinse your hair with egg and beer. It'll make it shiny, shimmery, and irresistible! Trust us when we tell you he won't be able to keep his hands off it.
- Paint your lips red. This will incite his animal instincts and draw attention to what you're saying. Make sure you ask him lots of questions about himself!
- Dab a little vanilla oil behind each ear. A way to a man's heart is through his stomach, and you just might be the tastiest treat he'll eat!
- Actually, most women aren't as tasty and fresh as

they'd like to be. To "sweeten the pot" once you've drawn him in, drink at least four cups of pineapple juice before you two decide to get jiggy. It'll keep him coming back for more!

• And finally, don't eat anything that can get stuck in your teeth. Stick to low-fat, low-carb, leaf-free dishes like carrots, boiled chicken, and lean steak. When he smiles at you, he doesn't want to see the broccoli grinning back!

I threw down the magazine, disgusted. Women had earned the right to vote in 1920 and seventy-some years later had apparently traded it in for the freedom to be cute. I walked over to the fridge for some cold water and spotted the Miller Lite in the back, a leftover from Sunny's tenure. Next to that was a carton with a half dozen brown eggs. I glanced from *Cosmo* back to the inside of my fridge.

Well, there was nothing wrong with having shiny hair, was there. And I wouldn't be doing it for Johnny. I'd be doing it for me.

I grabbed an egg and the beer, cracked both, and whipped them together in a bowl. I leaned over the kitchen sink and poured the slimy, fizzy mess onto my nearly dry head. The article hadn't mentioned how long to leave it in, so I stayed put for eleven—my lucky number—minutes. When I couldn't stand it any longer, I turned on the tap and rinsed out the glop until the water ran clear, and then bundled my hair into a towel turban.

In for a penny, in for a pound.

I rummaged through my makeup drawer and finally came up with some crusty old rouge that I dabbed on my lips. It was more liver pink than lover red, but maybe Stub's would be poorly lit. I had less luck finding vanilla oil. As a compromise, I grabbed the bottle of 100 percent vanilla extract from my spice rack and dabbed a little on each wrist and behind each ear. It was sticky, but I smelled like cookies. I knew I didn't have pineapple juice and wasn't going to order boiled chicken tonight, so I'd just have to stop at half–banana pants.

I was trying to regain some self-respect by reminding myself how I didn't want to date because all men went bad or died on me when Johnny pulled up. He'd been to my house once before, in June, to help me with some gardening. I thought we'd made a connection that night, but I was either too afraid or too smart to pursue it.

Would tonight tip that balance?

I let my hair out of the towel and brushed it. It was still damp but would dry quickly in the heat. I had visions of it plumping into a perfect sassy and sexy Barbarella do. I patted Tiger Pop and Luna goodbye and loped out to meet Johnny. He was leaning against the hood of his car, Adonis-like. He smiled when he saw me, the sun creating a halo of gold around his tanned face. He opened the passenger door for me, and I glided in. When he slid in his side, I could see his dimples carving out a little space on each cheek.

"What?" I asked.

"Nothing." His dimples deepened.

My pulse thudded in my wrists. Something about me had clearly amused him. That wasn't good. I was aiming for sexy, not silly. "What?" I repeated.

Johnny put the car into first and took off down the driveway. "You smell like a beer hall and have something yellow on your shoulder."

I glanced down, mortified. "Oh, um, it's a new shampoo. Beer shampoo. Beer and egg. Yolk."

He nodded as if I'd just said something reasonable. "Sounds good for your hair."

"I got it at the store." I swatted at a fly, but the movement of my wrist just attracted another.

"Are you OK if we eat at Stub's?" he asked.

"That'd be great." Suddenly, there was a swarm of heat-drunk flies hovering around me. Were they after the beer and egg in my hair? I swung again and caught a whiff of vanilla.

Fish sticks! I'd turned myself into fly bait. I might as well have rubbed some raw hamburger under each armpit and called it a night.

I shoved my vanilla-drenched hands under my legs and tried to wipe away the sweetness under each ear with my shoulder. Johnny watched out of the corner of his eye, a smile tugging at his mouth. When flies buzzed close, I blew at them out of the side of my mouth, hoping the radio covered up the sound. *Cosmo* was right, in a way: I sure was making a memorable impression on this first date.

As soon as we got inside Stub's, I excused myself to go to the bathroom. I was able to scour the vanilla and scrape most of the egg drippings off my shoulders. My hair, however, had dried and was now irreparably crusty. Fortunately, I always carried a hair band with me. Once I pulled my stiff do up and back and scrubbed the uneven, ailing pink off my lips, I felt slightly better. I still smelled like a beer hall, but at least I was *in* a beer hall.

Johnny was waiting for me at the bar, a teasing smile still playing across his lips. He didn't comment on my changed appearance. "I got us the last table, but they need to clear it off first. Can I get you a drink?"

I'd decided in the bathroom that this wasn't a date, if for no other reason than to save my sanity. Might as well stick with my plan of crossing number four off the *Cosmo* list. "A Coke with lemon would be nice."

The bartender nodded, and Johnny reached for his wallet. That's when Heaven, in all her clean-haired, immaculately made-up, youthful glory, appeared next to him.

"Johnny! I'm here with my brother's friends from college. They say they know you." Her smile was so beautiful it hurt to look at. "You should come sit with us!"

Johnny put his hand firmly on my waist. "Maybe another time. I'm with Mira."

My body tingled where he touched me. I quickly leaned over to the bartender. "Can you make that four cups of pineapple juice?"

Chapter 20

Johnny grabbed our drinks and let me lead the way into the dining room. Our table was relatively private, set back in a space like a closet with tied drapes instead of a door. We studied our menus inside the curtained alcove. We both ordered—steak for Johnny and ribs for me—before he told me the real reason he'd asked me out.

"I need a favor."

That didn't sound like one potential lover to another. I stared miserably at my hands, wondering if I'd indeed turned him off by ordering something meaty and messy.

"I'm going out of town for a few days, and I need someone to watch my place."

I hoped the confusion I felt hid the disappointment. "House-sit? But aren't you still at your mom's?"

When Johnny came over to help me garden in June, I had learned that he'd been looking at grad school in Wisconsin when he got word his dad was diagnosed with terminal stomach cancer. He returned to Battle Lake to help his mom take care of his dad and was making the best of his current life working at the nursery, giving piano lessons, teaching community ed classes, and being the town handyman. His dad had passed the end of June—it seemed like the entire town of Battle Lake had shown up to pay their respects—and Johnny was staying on another year to make sure his mom was situated. He was an only kid, like me.

"It's my cabin out on the west side of Silver Lake that I need watched. I think some kids are partying out there, spinning ueys in the driveway. The locks are still on the door, but I don't know for how long, especially if they get wind that I'm out of town."

I stared at the salad the waitress had slid in front of me. "Couldn't Jed watch it?"

Johnny rubbed his face. "Jed's a great guy, but not what you'd call reliable."

"Sure, no problem." Johnny and I were friends. That was it. He couldn't make it any clearer. "You just want me to drive out there every day?"

"Easier than that. All you need to do is keep your eyes peeled for a car with red paint on it."

I stopped with a cucumber slice halfway to my mouth. "Huh? A red car?"

"No, a car with red *on* it. I filled some balloons with paint and put them in the dried-up mud puddles in my driveway." He reached for the basket of bread. "They're covered with leaves. Anyone driving at night won't be able to see them. Whoever is tearing up the driveway is going to have a car full of red splatters."

That explained the bag of balloons I'd seen him buying earlier. I raised an eyebrow. "Isn't that a little vengeful for you?"

Johnny frowned. "My dad and I built that cabin. It's stood empty since I've been to college and he was sick, and I'm just getting it back in shape. I don't want it trashed."

My heart melted. "I'm sorry. Of course I'll watch for the red paint. You want me to call the police if I see something?"

"I want you to call me. I can be back within a few hours."

I thought about that. "Where are you going?"

The server filled our waters, distracting Johnny's gaze. "Wisconsin. Stevens Point, actually. To visit my grandma."

"Huh." I watched Johnny watching the waitress and wondered why he was suddenly unable to make eye contact with me. If I didn't know him better, I'd say that other than his genuine grief at losing his dad, he was telling me a big fat fib. I tried remembering where he'd told Dolly that his grandparents lived when he ran into us at the Fortune Café, but the beer fumes cloaking my head discouraged clear thinking.

Johnny nodded. "Yup."

"When are you leaving?"

"Tonight. When we're done with supper."

This was getting stranger. "On the Fourth of July? What's the rush?"

Johnny rubbed his palms on his pants. "Sure is taking our food a long time."

"Sure is."

"Yup."

"Yup," I said, refusing to fill in the silence any more than that. He looked so uncomfortable that I wanted to help him out, but not as much as I wanted to find out what he was hiding.

"Yeah, no rush, really," he finally said. "I just thought I'd go see my grandma tonight, beat the weekend traffic. Can we talk about something else?"

What I wanted to talk about was how Johnny was turning into a great big liar, just like the rest. Instead, I sipped at my saccharine-sweet pineapple juice and wondered if his uneasiness had anything to do with the missing Chief Wenonga, the bloody scalp, or the mislaid Mr. Myers.

I made myself a promise to check out Johnny's cabin and see what this booby-trapping paint-balloon dealio was really about in the very near future.

Chapter 21

My nondate supper finished uneventfully. Johnny drove me home. He flashed me a peculiar smile when he opened my car door. It was probably just the beer fumes still wafting from my tapped keg of hair turning his stomach. As we said our goodbyes, he told me he'd check in with me when he returned if I didn't call him on his cell first.

I considered biking to the fireworks at Glendalough Park to keep a low profile. However, Fourth of July traffic was notoriously dangerous. People were excited, drunk, and staring at the sky. It was a bad time to be on two wheels, so I reluctantly hopped in my Toyota, hoping the gravel dust would make it indistinguishable from other cars in the deepening dusk. With my windows down, I could hear the frogs sighing and the crickets singing in the fragrant sloughs hugging the road. The cooling evening breeze felt like a soft kiss on the baby hairs of my neck, and despite all my worries, I began to grow excited about the upcoming fireworks.

My family had rarely made it to the Fourth of July festivities when I was younger. My dad was usually drunk by dark, and before I hit ten, my mom started going to bed early to avoid him. I ended up spending nearly every Fourth perched on the slouched metal roof of the storage shed on our tiny hobby farm in the middle of the flat west-central Minnesota prairie. I couldn't see the real fireworks streaking through the sky above Lake Koronis, six miles away, but I could hear them, and I could see our neighbors shoot off roman candles smuggled in from

North Dakota. Every time I heard a pop, I'd throw handfuls of tree helicopters or grass clippings into the air.

I soon outgrew the Fourth of July on the roof and was left to watch fireworks on the little black-and-white TV in our living room for as long as I could put up with my dad's drunken commentary on everything from his terrible time in Vietnam to the woman he'd met there, the one he should have married instead of my mom. Now, as a grown-up, watching real fireworks was like reclaiming the childhood I never had.

I knew parking would be impossible in Glendalough and even worse trying to leave after the show, so I joined a sprinkling of cars parking just outside the entrance. I fell in line with the crowds streaming toward prime viewing spots.

I spotted Dolly on the far side of the large state park map and interpretive sign. She still had the lighthearted step and distant smile of a happy woman. I was about to holler a greeting when I noticed Les hot on her heels. He likely imagined he was blending in with the crowd, but with the angry set of his shoulders and the grimace on his face, he stood out like a snake in a baby crib. When Dolly stopped abruptly to touch a wild lily sprouting up amid the prairie grass, Les also halted and dropped down, pretending to tie his shoe. Did Dolly know she was being tailed, and why was Les following her?

I was about to become the third car on that train when Gina popped up alongside me.

"There you are!" she said. "When did you get here?"

She wore a shapeless patriotic T-shirt, blue jeans, and flip-flops. Her blonde hair was scraped back in a ponytail, and her bright green eyes sparkled.

"Just now," I said, noting the Diet Sprite she held. That surprised me. Gina was a drinker. Maybe she'd mixed gin in the bottle. "So, what's your big news?"

"Let's walk and talk." She hooked her arm through mine and navigated us around the jostling crowds toward a choice spot on the banks of Molly Stark.

"We're walking, but we're not talking." I was studying the crowds, trying to catch a glimpse of Dolly, but I wasn't oblivious to the fact that Gina was unusually quiet.

She stopped dead in her tracks and faced me. "OK, Mira, don't be mad at me, but I'm pregnant."

My initial thought was *ohmygod, better you than me*, but my sporadically effective social filter managed to click down in the nick of time. I grabbed her up in a big hug. "Mad? Why would I be mad? You're going to be a fantastic mom!"

Gina laughed and pushed me off. "I know how you feel about Leif, but he's changed. He swore he'll never cheat again. He's excited for the baby."

My eyes misted over. I didn't know whether Leif had or would change, but I knew that Gina was a whole lot braver than I'd ever be. "I'm sure he *is* excited. I hope this is everything you want it to be."

Gina squeezed my hand, sniffing at the air. "Did someone spill a beer on you? You reek."

"New shampoo."

"You know, Mir," she said, leaning close, "they say pregnancy is contagious. Once one friend gets it, they all do." Her tone was teasing. "You're on birth control, right?"

"Ha!" I considered my Battle Lake dating options, which took all of a half second. "That'd be like wearing a parachute while you're driving." I pointed. "Is that Leif over there?"

We wove through the crowd to the blanket he'd set out for the three of us. I said hello and was introduced to the two couples Gina and Leif had come with. From what I could tell from a first glance, both were from heavy-drinking and TV-watching stock, the women sporting '80s claw bangs and the men both condescending and dumb. It was only an odd combination if you'd never been west of the Twin Cities. I'd tolerated the type when I had to, but when one of the guys, who was coincidentally sporting a Long Hard Johnson Fishing Poles T-shirt, asked Leif if he'd ever heard the joke about how you couldn't rely on a woman because you should never trust anything that could bleed for seven days and not die, I decided it was time to search for greener pastures.

I stood, brushed myself off, and hugged Gina goodbye. It was going to be hard to locate Dolly among the crowd since it'd grown dark. Hundreds of blankets covered with couples and families dotted the shoreline. No alcohol was allowed within the park limits, but people were openly swigging beer and frosty wine coolers. I decided it'd be the best use of my time to hit the far end of the lakeshore and work my way back inward, walking along the beach and then backtracking one layer in, until I'd worked myself between every group of people. Of course, I'd only find Dolly if she'd situated herself in this prime firework-viewing location. If she wasn't on Molly Stark, or if Les had knocked her over the head and dragged her into the woods, I was SOL.

I caught snatches of conversation as I walked through the crowds, punctuated by the first sparkling fireworks lighting up the sky.

"Oooh! That looked like a purple mushroom!"

"When I was a kid, the fireworks blew up in shapes, like flags or George Washington's profile."

"Did you bring the Boone's Farm?"

"You gotta emphasize the 'Boone's,' not the 'Farm,' man, or it just sounds gross."

"Wow! That lit up the whole night!"

"Think they'll have one shaped like Chief Wenonga?"

I reached the far end of the crowd, trying not to get distracted by the beautiful rainbow reflections shimmering on the lake. It was when I was pulling my gaze away from the water that I caught sight of a couple, thirty feet up the shore on a little stretch of beach almost too narrow to stand on, the water crowding one side and marshy reeds on the other. I waited for the next explosion to light up the sky before I could see who it was. In a flash of brilliant red, white, and blue, I clearly made out Dolly's signature reddish-blonde hair and the dark silhouette of a tattoo on her right wrist, but the person standing next to her was obscured in shadows.

It was a masculine figure, taller than Dolly, leaning down to talk to her. Whether his hair was light or dark, I couldn't tell. Either way, Dolly was happy to have him close, so I was pretty sure it wasn't Les, who was shorter than Dolly anyway. I casually strolled closer, dropping down on my haunches when Dolly glanced my way. When I reached the edge of the reeds, about twenty feet from where the couple stood and away from the bulk of the fireworks crowd, I could make out bits of conversation.

". . . for another week or so."

"You sure that's right?"

"I'm positive." Dolly's deep chuckle. "You think I have what it takes?"

". . . up to you . . ."

I risked a peek around the reeds. Dolly's back was to me, but her companion was looking in my direction. I quickly darted back behind the reeds, but not before Johnny's eyes locked on mine.

"Mira?" he called out, but I was already jogging toward my car, brushing hot tears off my cheeks.

Chapter 22

Sad almost immediately morphed into furious.

I was mad at Johnny for not being in love with me, even though he was turning out to be a sneak, and I was angry at Dolly for horning in on my territory. The argument could be made that she didn't know I was interested in Johnny, but I wasn't in the mood for generosity. Mostly, though, I was pissed at myself for falling for another guy. Love always ended badly for me, I knew that, and still I'd let my heart slide toward Johnny. I couldn't even fall for a fiberglass statue without it producing tragedy, for the love of Betsy.

I was so caught up in my dark mood that I didn't notice Brando stroll out of the woods. I walked smack into him.

"Oh! Sorry." This was my first face-to-face encounter with him, and based on the carnivorous once-over he gave me, he seemed to be enjoying it a great deal more than I was.

"Not a problem." He grinned. "Where are you going in such a hurry?"

"I'm not a big fan of fireworks," I lied.

"Mmm." He beckoned over my shoulder. "Something interesting back there?"

His tone made the question feel dangerous. From where we stood, I could see the outlines of hundreds of people staring up at the sky over by the beach, but there was no foot traffic near us, and the closest blanket of people was a few hundred yards away. Feeling slightly uneasy, I swatted at a mosquito and went from defense to offense.

"Just bright lights in the sky." I wiped at my face, erasing the last of the tears. "What about you? What were you doing in the woods?"

He held out his hand. "I don't think we've met. I'm Brando Erikkson. I'm in town for the festivities."

I shook his hand reluctantly. "Mira James."

A light of recognition flared in his eyes. "Sure. You've got that column. Kennie mentioned you."

I'll bet. "You didn't answer my question. You see anything interesting back there?"

He shrugged. "Not much. There's a path down to the lake, the direction you just came from, as a matter of fact, but some young lovers were making the most of the night, so I circled back through the woods."

Ouch. "Well, it was nice meeting you."

"Some of us are having a party after the show. You should join us." He laid a light hand on my shoulder. "Maybe you could do an article on me."

"Yeah, maybe." I pushed his hand off and stomped away. The party would probably be a good place to gather more information on the missing Chief, but I was in no mood. I located my car without spotting any cops and rolled home.

Chapter 23

I fell into a funky sleep and awoke to a bright, shining fifth of July, my head pounding from a broken-heart hangover. I didn't feel like eating breakfast, or cleaning, or watching TV, or gardening, or doing anything else I normally did to pull myself out of a dark place.

That left only mowing the lawn, all one and a half acres.

What I most enjoyed about cutting the grass was the clean smell of fresh-cut lawn and the soft, trimmed carpet of green afterward. I strolled down to the outbuilding where I stored the mower, listening to fuzzy bumblebees the size of peanut M&M's bumping against the petals of my summer flowers. I gassed up the old Snapper rider, checked the oil, and yanked the whipcord. The engine fired immediately, and I began the bumpy job.

First, I mowed the area between the silo, barn, and two sheds. Then I trimmed the strip running parallel to the mile-long driveway and the tiny beach area down by the lake, and I ended by clearing off the wide section circumscribing the house, ducking low to avoid the branches on the far perimeter.

As I mowed, I let my mind drift.

My world had been turned upside down in less than a week. The strangeness had come with this intense, portentous heat, and there was no end in sight. First, Kennie had returned from hush-hush training the middle of last week, which I now knew had been her radical cheer-leading camp. Then, at the planning meeting the next day, Dolly and

Les interrupted the proceedings with their wild talk about getting rid of Chief Wenonga. Lo and behold, the next morning the Chief disappeared, and someone left behind a bloody chunk of head. That very day, an angry Gary Wohnt showed up at the library looking for me, a first. Throw into that mix a missing Native American impersonator from yesterday's parade, and it all became too weird for words.

Dolly and Les were the most likely suspects, but I didn't like the smell of Brando Erikkson on the scene, especially since he was somehow connected to Les. I knew where those two were at the time the parade mascot disappeared, though, so that put Dolly on the hook as suspect number one. I experienced a cheap thrill at the idea of pinning her as the culprit, but it was too easy. If you were going to steal two Native American representations, why broadcast your position at a well-attended town meeting? If it were a publicity stunt, she would have claimed it by now—unless she had something else planned, a Native American–stealing trifecta.

I returned to my other burning question: How did a twenty-three-foot statue disappear under the cover of night? The Battle Lake cops trolled the main drag at least once every hour, so whoever took Chief Wenonga must be a pretty quick statue dismantler, which would point the finger squarely at Brando. But why would he steal it? He had a whole pile of 'em back in Wisconsin. It made more sense that Les, who had made a name for himself flouting authority, would've removed the Chief. He certainly had access to the big equipment I would imagine was necessary—his brother owned a construction company in Perham.

Two hours of mowing, and I was hot and sticky all over but had no answers. It wouldn't be easy, but I needed to track down the Chief to find his abductor, and that's all there was to it. A good place to start would be to interview the people who lived in the handful of houses surrounding Halverson Park to see if they'd seen or heard anything suspicious the night the Chief disappeared.

That would be my next step.

After that, I'd visit Johnny's cabin, though the idea unsettled me. What game was he playing, asking me to watch his place, lying about leaving town immediately, and meeting up secretly with Dolly at the fireworks? Dink.

I parked the mower and walked on shaky legs back to the house. I considered taking another shower before I left but decided there was no point. Johnny had moved on. The Chief was gone. Who was I trying to impress?

I hosed the grass flecks off my legs, turned the spray on the garden to refresh my vegetables, rinsed my face and hands in the chute of water, and hopped on my bike. The smell of two-stroke gasoline lingered on me and became cloying in the concentrated heat of the midday sun, but I couldn't pedal fast enough to escape it. By the time I reached Halverson Park, I was sweaty and flushed. The good news was that the 30K bike race and 5K run were scheduled for today, so there were a lot of sweaty and flushed people around to provide cover.

When I strolled toward Halverson, my bike at my side, I realized my luck was holding out. The tiny 1950s square blue box of a home nearest the park was holding a garage sale. I kickstanded my bike, sauntered up the driveway, and rummaged through a pile of old record albums, pausing to admire the bright cover of Engelbert Humperdinck's *After the Lovin'*. Next to me stood two older ladies I didn't recognize.

"Isn't this yours?" The white-haired woman nearest me used a lot of her face when she talked. She held out a worn *Doubleday Cookbook* roughly the size of a wheelbarrow toward her friend.

"My name on the inside cover?" the second woman asked.

The white-haired woman opened it up. "Yup. Trudie Johannsen, 1952."

"Well, I'll be damned. I sold that at last year's all-town garage sale."

"You want it back?"

She studied the book. "How much is it?"

"Two dollars."

"Judas in a cup! I can hardly pass up a deal like that. Give it over."

As they discussed haggling for a lower price, I grabbed a frizzed-out hair tie with a nickel sticker on it and walked up to the scowling lady sitting at the card table, a steel box full of change in front of her. "Can I buy this hair tie?" I asked.

"If it's got a sticker on it, you can buy it."

I handed her a nickel and shoved the band into my pocket. "It must be weird not having Chief Wenonga to look at anymore." I gestured toward the park.

The woman glanced over at the Chief's former home, then back at me. She adjusted herself in the chair, one polyester-clad thigh creating a sucking vacuum against the other. I noticed her eyebrows were overplucked and hung above each eye like a gray toenail clipping. "You want to buy anything else?"

I glanced around and reached for a half-full bottle of perfume next to her. "How much is this?"

"Fifty cents."

I gave her a dollar and waited for change. "I don't suppose you saw what happened?"

"Don't suppose. By the time I looked out, all there was to see was a girl standing there, her hands on the post." She jabbed her thumb in the general direction of where the Chief statue had stood as she stared down into her change box. "Looked an awful lot like you."

I sucked in a quick little breath. "Really? Wouldn't that be hard to tell from this far away?"

"I got eyes like an eagle. You wouldn't want to buy that Vikings helmet, would you? Cris Carter wore it in 1996."

I looked at the beaten-up purple-and-gold football helmet and sighed. "How much?"

"Twenty dollars. Cris Carter wore it in 1996."

"Mm-hmm. You mentioned that." I dug through my pockets for a bigger bill. "There's a lot of women who look like me around, don't you think?"

"I think it depends on whether or not you want that helmet."

"Sold." I traded her a twenty for a helmet full of a stranger's sweat and hightailed it out of there before she extorted more cash.

I didn't have any more luck at the next house over, or the next. At the fourth house, though, I learned that the owner had seen a car leaving Halverson Park early the morning the Chief disappeared. My heart soared until I was told the car was a small brown Toyota. At least two people had spotted either my car or me at the scene of the crime. Now I knew beyond a doubt why Gary Wohnt was after me. Stomach acid was punching its way up my throat.

Since no clues were forthcoming in this neighborhood, I hopped on my bike and pedaled out to Johnny's Silver Lake cabin a mile and a half north. Silver Lake was small and clean, but the west side was swamp, so only the east side had cabins. I pedaled the flat stretch, coasting when I reached the populated side so I could read the mailboxes. Sweat raced between my shoulder blades, and I vowed to invest in some aluminum-laced, heavy-duty deodorant and antiperspirant next time I was in the apothecary. This sweltering heat wasn't gonna let up.

I couldn't find Johnny's last name printed on any of the mailboxes. I was about to give up when I noticed the dirt road snaking up into the woods to my left. I followed the trail to a handful of tucked-away rustic structures, so close together and similar they looked almost like an abandoned resort. The cabin farthest from the entry road and closest to the lake had a black mailbox at the end of its driveway with LEESON painted in bronze on it.

As I drew closer to the cabin, a hot breeze kicked through the treetops, creating a scary whisper in the popple leaves. It was otherwise spooky quiet back here, except for the distant drone of an Evinrude. The other cabins appeared unoccupied from where I stood.

I parked my bike, stripped off my T-shirt, and used it to wipe the sweat off my neck and chest. Standing in a sports bra and shorts, I wondered if it was a good idea to continue. No one knew where I was, and Battle Lake hadn't been a safe place lately. I tucked my T-shirt in my waistband and planted my hands on my hips, forcing myself to gather up some nerve. It was daylight, bright as a new penny, and nothing bad happened when the sun was out.

Seven long strides and I reached a low spot in the driveway. If there was a storm, this would be where a puddle would form. Right now, though, it didn't look like it had rained in this spot. It looked like a deer had been gutted and dressed out. The brown winter leaves—probably carted in from the woods by Johnny—were smeared in crusty red gore. Judging by the amount of splatter, his plan to tag his trespasser's vehicle had worked.

I grabbed a stick and poked at the pile until I dug up a white piece of rubber, stained crimson—one of the balloons. When I pulled my stick back, it was also smeared with red. Some of the paint was still wet. Whoever had driven over the balloons had likely done so within the past twelve hours or so.

I followed the faint red tire tracks leading toward the cabin, careful to stick to the clear, dry sections of road. My senses were hyper-tuned. I was sure that whoever had been out here messing around was gone, but I didn't know what they'd left behind.

Chapter 24

The cabin itself looked small, maybe two big rooms inside, and the door must face the lake, because I couldn't see it. The outside was covered in stained wood siding with a brown shake roof. It blended in nicely with the forest and was probably a great place to trespass and party if a person didn't know that Johnny was checking on it regularly.

I peered through the window nearest me, the one facing the driveway, and saw that there was in fact only one open room inside, containing a small kitchen, a bed, and steps to a loft. There was a door off that, and judging from the cabin's dimensions, it could only lead to a small bathroom. The bed appeared rumpled and muddy.

More pressing, however, was the amount of light being let in through the wide-open door on the lake side of the cabin.

Johnny had been right to worry. Someone had broken in.

A loon wailed its haunted call as I pushed through the raspberry brambles, wondering why it was that people rarely did for themselves—landscapers had the messiest yards, chefs rarely ate at home, and carpenters' houses were never finished.

When I reached the side of the cabin facing Silver Lake, the condition of the door startled me. It wasn't just open. It *dangled*, only one hinge left to secure it to the frame, and its lock and handle had been obliterated. Wood splinters were strewn on the ground.

A pine scent laced with sawdust, mildew, and something disturbing that I couldn't quite place washed out of the cabin. The trespassing partiers had probably peed in a corner. *Jerks.*

I swiped at the mosquitoes buzzing around my exposed skin—the little beasties were driving me up a wall—and took a deep breath before going in. The inside of the cabin was surprisingly neat except for the lumpy bed in the shadows. The main room was maybe twenty feet by twenty feet, and all the kitchen cupboards were closed. There were no dishes in the sink. I figured the smell must be coming from the bathroom, but when I pushed open the door, careful not to leave prints, there was only a simple white toilet, the lid up and water clean, and a matching pedestal sink.

I sighed. The wretched smell must be coming from the bed. I'd avoided examining it too closely because my fear was that Johnny's cabin bed had become the local lovers' lane, and I was in no hurry to check that out up close. I'd come this far, though, and I might as well see her through. The rotting scent became overwhelming as I neared the bed, and my inner alarms were going off, telling me to run. I pushed through.

When I reached the bed, I wished I hadn't.

The sheets and blankets were rumpled like ocean waves, stained with pools of maroon so dark it was almost black. Was this more paint? A nightstand stood between the bed and the wall, a quilt shoved in the space next to it.

When I leaned over to grab the blanket, I realized it was wearing a blood-crusted T-shirt, blue jeans, and one shoe. The other foot was bare and stiff from death, its sheer whiteness the most disturbing sight. I blinked, but the image stayed behind my eyelids: that icy pale foot, sprinkled with wiry black toe hair.

I couldn't bring myself to look at the head.

I covered my nose, trying to stem the tide of nausea surfing on the musty smell of cabin and woods mixed with the heavy iron scent of violent death. The room fell sideways, and I kept myself upright by lurching the opposite way. The humming in my ears made it impossible to think. I stumbled out of the cabin, swallowing furiously to keep from throwing up. I couldn't leave any trace of me in this nightmare butcher shop.

Outside, I gulped in the fresh air of the forest, tears streaming down my face.

Johnny's cabin housed a corpse. What the hell was going on?

Chapter 25

I biked home dazed and hollow, then showered on weak knees, scrubbing my skin until it was raw, before driving to my pay phone of choice for making 911 calls. I watched as if from a distance, my hands trembling as I punched in numbers to report the body at Johnny's cabin. I gave the location and situation but no details, not even my fake name. Afterward, I cruised to Gina's house, no longer caring if Wohnt saw me.

She wasn't home, so I let myself in and helped myself to a glass of vodka on ice.

It'd been my dad's favorite drink, minus the ice.

I now understood where a person could get used to drinking straight liquor. The slightly medicinal bite felt good going down, disinfecting my memories and blotting out dark thoughts.

By my second glass, I was beginning to feel in control again. Either someone had been murdered in Johnny's cabin without his knowledge, or—and I didn't want to think this but facts were facts—Johnny and Dolly had killed a guy, hidden the corpse, and set me up to take the fall. Well, if so, I'd outsmarted them. No one knew I'd visited the cabin, and the police were going to find the body and nail those two. I couldn't really blame them for choosing me as their patsy, if that's what'd happened. Finding dead bodies had turned into one of my primary occupations around here, so I had good references.

The mellow, sane part of my brain was telling me that was ludicrous, that Johnny was no killer, that he'd never manipulate me like that. I poured cold vodka over that part of my brain, drowning it. What did I really know about Johnny, other than he was sexy and put on a good show of being a nice guy? Well, I was done falling for it. I didn't need *anybody*. I was just fine being alone.

No one could betray me if I only counted on myself.

I drunk-dozed for a while and was awakened by my stomach's fierce growling. Now that I had my future as a monk in order, going to the Fortune Café for a late lunch seemed like a grand idea. I stumbled out the door, wondering when it'd gotten so damn hot outside. Certain that my car ignition had turned into the bake switch on an oven, I decided to walk. I'd traipsed almost to the front door of the café, bobbing and weaving, when I felt an ominous presence loom behind me, blocking out the sweltering July sun.

I turned.

A steely-eyed Gary Wohnt was staring me down. I should have been terrified, but instead felt delightfully numb.

"I've been looking for you," he said.

He was so muscular, so imposing, that he'd always intimidated me. Thank vodka I no longer cared about anything. I swayed slightly, then fixed him with an imperious stare. I had to squint one eye to do it. "Gary."

He blinked. Waited a beat. "Where are you going?"

Answer nothing, deny everything, make counter accusations. "Where are *you* going?"

His cheek twitched, and then he sighed. "I need you to come to the station to answer some questions, Ms. James."

I heard a faint siren. I was about to glance around when I realized it was my internal warning bell I was hearing. It had been important to avoid Gary, and it still was, but I'd lost my thinking beans. I needed to buy time until I could gather them back up. "OK, well, I'm free later this afternoon, maybe around four?"

"Now," he growled.

Good sense, and with it, fear, was finally returning, reminding me why I shouldn't drink. "Can't we just talk here?"

"I don't think you want that."

"Fine." I tossed my head with what I hoped was arrogant inno-cence, but to tell the truth, I was beginning to feel a little green around the gills. Gary Wohnt and I walked without speaking the two blocks to the Battle Lake Police Station. The three-room brick building was stifling. The open windows allowed in pizza-oven hot air, and the lazy ceiling fan circulated it down into my face.

"Why don't you have a seat, Ms. James." Despite the wording, it was not a question.

I pulled up a metal chair with a screech and dropped down so I was facing him across his desk. I was going to outlast him. He had nothing on me. I would stare him down, one mask of control to another. We might be here for days, but I would not talk.

"I didn't take Wenonga." The words spilled out like water. "I was only there on Friday morning because I noticed he was gone. I was going to tell you, but I was worried you'd think I had something to do with stealing him. I wouldn't steal him. I loved him. Those *were* my fingerprints on the one post, but that was an accident."

Dammit.

Wohnt sighed and closed his eyes for ten long seconds, his fingers tenting over the bridge of his nose. "That's not why I asked you to come here today, Ms. James. You are here because two hours ago, a dead body was found in Jonathan Leeson's cabin on Silver Lake, and you were the last confirmed person seen in Mr. Leeson's company."

Shoot. He was up to date. "Why aren't you out there now?"

"There are officers on the scene. In fact, the FBI has been called in. I'd like to present as much information as possible to them when they arrive. You can help me with that." He leaned back in his chair, but his posture did not relax an inch. "Do you know where Mr. Leeson is right now?"

I knew where he'd told me he was going to be. Visiting his grandma in Stevens Point. However, I was suddenly sure that was not where he was. "Did you ask his mom?"

He picked up a pen and turned it over in his hands. "Mrs. Leeson said she believed her son was staying at the cabin for the night and doesn't know his current whereabouts."

"Do you know whose body it is?"

My pivot didn't throw him. "We haven't positively identified the body. What did you and Mr. Leeson visit about at Stub's last night?"

Who'd told on me? "Ummm, gardening mostly."

He put down the pen and drilled me with his dark eyes. "Are you dating Mr. Leeson?"

I snorted involuntarily. "No."

He seemed to consider this. "I think it'd be best if you submitted a set of your fingerprints."

My mouth went dry. "Right now?"

"Yes."

"Do I have to?"

"We would look favorably upon it if you did."

"Do I have to?" I repeated.

"I highly recommend it."

"Do I have to?" I could do this all day.

His mouth formed a straight line. "No."

I took a deep breath. This confrontation had sobered me considerably. "Then I think I'd like to leave. OK?"

He clenched his jaw, and his cheekbones popped. "Don't go far."

I stood shakily but quickly, worried that Wohnt was going to change his mind about letting me leave but unable to stop the question leaking out of my mouth. "The body you found. Was it Randy Myers?"

He shook his head. "No."

I nodded. "Was it missing part of its scalp?"

Gary Wohnt had closed his eyes again, so I couldn't tell what he was thinking, but for a second, I thought I heard an edge of respect in his voice. "Yes. It was."

Chapter 26

As I pushed outside into the hairy wall of heat, my head was reeling and my stomach churning. It wasn't until I entered the Fortune Café that I started to get a grip. The cool air laced with ginger and chocolate brought my anxiety down a notch. I *would* get to the bottom of this. The entire situation had become a steaming latrine—the scalp-deficient body at Johnny's was obviously connected to Chief Wenonga's disappearance—and I needed to fix it. Not to save anyone else, mind you, but for my own peace of mind and so the cops would leave me alone.

I'd locate the Chief, and Randy Myers, and discover why someone had left a body at Johnny's cabin. (I still wasn't ruling out the possibility that Dolly and Johnny had left it for me to find.) Those who'd messed up would pay. I squared my shoulders and strode up to the counter and directly into the lusty path of Brando Erikkson's gaze. He stood from his two-chair table.

"Mira! Two run-ins in under twenty-four hours. Fate must be bringing us together."

"It's a small town," I said, *so* not in the mood to flirt. "It's gravity bringing us together."

He chuckled and indicated his table. "Join me?"

I glanced around the café. It was lunch rush, and there were no empty tables. I poked my head around the corner to the game room and library and still saw no place to sit. I considered ordering a bucket of coffee to go but reminded myself of my newfound commitment to get to the bottom of things. That included talking to Brando to find out what he knew. I might as well do it in public, in the daylight. "Sure."

I started to walk toward the counter, but Brando put his hand on my arm. "I'll get it. What would you like?"

I paused reluctantly. "An iced coffee and a cinnamon scone would be fine, thank you." I grudgingly admired his seriously tight rear as he walked toward the counter. Too bad he gave me the creeps. I took the opportunity to serve myself several glasses of water from the serve-yourself pitcher. The cool liquid felt like balm sliding down my throat, diluting my bellyful of vodka. I made my way back to his table, everything feeling so surreal.

"Here you go." Brando set the coffee and scone in front of me, but instead of sitting, he remained standing, leaning his hip into the table. *Whatever, weirdo.*

"Thanks." I sat and sipped the sweet, cool coffee and felt it slice through the remaining fog surrounding my brain.

Brando watched me drink, a tight smile on his face. "You didn't come to my party last night."

"I was tired." I closed my eyes for several seconds and enjoyed my increased focus. "I went home."

"Too bad. It was a great time. Good music, good drinks, hot men." I opened my eyes in time to see him wink, then stretch his hands over his head like a cat in a sunbeam.

I took another glug. I might need to order a second one. I reached for the scone. "Great."

"Yes, this is a nice little town you have here. The woodchuck is going to fit in real nice."

I coughed on a piece of scone. "I was going to ask you about that. Why a woodchuck?"

Brando smirked and ran a hand sinuously up his thigh before stroking his chest through his shirt. Next, he placed a foot on his chair, offering me an unbroken view of his testicle cleavage. I was wondering if he was about to ask me to cup his balls when I realized what he was doing: flirting with himself, with me as his audience.

Ew.

"Can you please sit down?" I asked, my appetite gone. "It's hard to talk to you when you're standing."

Brando appeared slightly taken aback, and then disappointed, but he plunked into his chair. "You're a feisty one."

"'Bitter' is probably more accurate." I rubbed my nose. "So why the woodchuck? Why not another Chief Wenonga?"

He tossed his glossy black hair to the side. "Too costly. We start out with a single statue mold for all the large men—your Paul Bunyans, Muffler Men, Carolina Cowboy, Jesus Christs. Then, usually all we have to do is dress them for the part and place an object in their hands. You know, axes or crosses, that sort of thing. The Indian line is different, though. We had to build a whole new chest and arms for those, plus the headdress. It's so time-consuming that we don't even make them anymore. In fact, we only produced three statues out of that Chief Wenonga mold."

I considered what he'd said and came up with a single conclusion. "You're in a weird line of work."

Brando shook his head in disagreement. "Not at all! My dad started out building boats in Wisconsin, but we needed something to do during the off-season, so he started making the statues. The work was crude at first, but now it's art. I don't sell anything that isn't absolutely perfect."

I finished my coffee. "Which is why you're giving away the woodchuck?"

He shrugged. "Its face melted a little. You can hardly tell when you're driving past."

I grimaced. "And when will this huge, deformed woodchuck be arriving in Battle Lake?"

"It's on its way as we speak." He glanced around the room as if bored with our conversation. "It's being driven over from Stevens Point, Wisconsin."

Click.

Last night Johnny had told me he was visiting his grandma in Stevens Point. Brando's company was in Stevens Point. Too much coincidence. "You know Johnny Leeson?"

Brando considered. "The albino guy in that band? The one with the brother? Sure, I like their stuff." He took the opportunity to slide his hand across the table and onto my arm.

"Not Johnny *Winter.*" I wrenched my arm out of reach. "Johnny *Leeson.* He's from Battle Lake."

Brando shook his head. "Never heard of him."

He seemed to be telling the truth. I got the distinct impression Brando didn't pay much attention to men, but he'd remember one he'd consider competition in the looks department. "So how long does it take to dismantle a statue like Chief Wenonga?"

Brando's eyes flashed sharply, so quickly that I might have imagined it, and then went back to a relaxed, half-lidded state. "I don't know. I'm an artist, not a construction worker. Before that, I had a thriving modeling career."

If his reference to modeling was meant to impress me, it was a wasted effort. "If you design the statues, you must have some idea of how they come apart."

He sighed and leaned back heavily in his chair, appearing bored again. "You only have one-note women in this town? That Kennie Rogers is about as interesting as hemorrhoid surgery, too. Sloppy kisser, by the way."

Heat rose in my chest and my head suddenly felt tight. I wasn't signing up for Kennie's fan club anytime soon, but knocking her was my job, not his. "You can say a lot of things about Kennie, but the woman is *not* boring," I said. "And you know what's a million times worse than a sloppy kisser? A man who kisses and tells."

The front door jingled, and Brittany and Heaven sashayed in. Brando's eyes were on them like metal on a magnet, rendering me immediately invisible.

Might as well take advantage.

"So, you have *no* idea how to take a fiberglass statue apart?" I asked.

His eyes remained trained on the new arrivals, but his ego stayed with me. "*Of course* I know how. I own the company. Like I said, the statues are made from fiberglass in open molds. Then we bond the seams together, and you've got a statue. We set them up; we don't take them down."

"Never?" I prodded. "You *never* take them down?"

"Huh?" He was still watching Brittany and Heaven, his expression distracted. I realized that from the side, he was a dead ringer for a dark-eyed, dark-haired Matthew McConaughey.

Brittany and Heaven had sauntered to the counter and were bent over the baked goods display case, their Daisy Dukes magically covering their lower-ass shelf. Or maybe they didn't have lower-ass shelves. Suddenly angry, I leaned forward. "You've *never* taken a statue down?"

"No. Never." Brando kept his gaze on the eye candy, a leer on his well-formed lips. "Because you'd need a wrecking ball for that. There's no way to take one of those statues down without destroying it."

Chapter 27

Uff da meda.

Until now, I'd assumed that Chief Wenonga had been statue-napped and was being held in a warehouse somewhere, or maybe an empty silo, whole and perhaps missing me.

Brando Erikkson's careless words had crushed that dream.

I needed to face facts: Chief Wenonga was gone, never to return. I tried that reality on for size for thirty whole seconds before choosing to reject. Brando was still ogling Brittany's and Heaven's behinds.

"You're kinda awful, but thanks for the coffee and scone," I said. "I'm gonna head."

He didn't even twitch. I don't think he'd have noticed I left if I hadn't swung by to say goodbye to Sid, blocking his view of Brittany and Heaven long enough for them to order. No one was gonna eye-stalk on my watch. After, I whisked myself through the coffee shop door, happy in my decision to believe the Chief was still whole. My made-from-scratch reality was going to win this one. Underneath my bravado, however, I was hurting. Johnny lying to me, the dead body, backsliding on my commitment to quit drinking the second the going got tough, Gary questioning me. I felt exposed, numb.

Alone.

I needed to clear my head, and that meant only one thing: gardening. Unfortunately, the Fates had a different plan for me.

"Mira James! Just the girl we need." Kennie grabbed me just as I stepped into the blazing sun. She was surrounded by a hopeful-looking crowd.

I stared, confused.

"Gary Wohnt was supposed to help me judge the pets and owners look-alike contest," she continued, "but he got called away. You can fill in for him and write a neat little article for the *Recall* while you're at it."

I shook my head so vehemently that something wobbled loose. "No. Absolutely not. I have plans."

"Twenty minutes, that's all we need," Kennie sang, smiling down at me from the teetering heights of her four-inch espadrilles.

"What about all these people?" I gestured at the crowd behind her.

"Friends and family of the pet owners, and therefore not eligible to judge. Come on. Twenty minutes, I cross my heart and hope to cry. And *phoo-ee*, do you smell like a sweaty wino. I'm gonna have to come over later and do you a favor."

That threat was so ominous that my mouth clicked shut until Kennie dragged me to the spot where the turtle races were usually held. The mob followed along, apparently relieved that their loved ones were going to get a chance to be judged for how much they looked like their animals. Kennie shoved a pad into my hand.

"You and I need to agree on a score between one and ten," she said, "with ten being the strongest resemblance."

"Fine. Let's get it done and over with." There were only ten names on the pad. According to the tally, six of them were dog owners, one owned a ferret, one had a fish, and two owned cats.

We walked up to the contestants, both animals and owners drooping in the blazing afternoon heat. Kennie cooed at how cute the pets were while I wondered whether people chose animals who looked like them or whether we all just started looking like our pets after a while. If so, I was hoping for some Tiger Pop highlights.

"Well, aren't you just the sweetest!" Kennie stopped to pet a chunk-a-lunky golden retriever named Kasey. Next to Kasey was a pleasantly chubby blond man with friendly bags under his eyes wearing a brass-colored shirt. When the dog blinked, the man blinked. The two even had matching jowls. Kennie and I exchanged an astonished look before both writing down a ten.

Next was a man holding a five-inch bluegill on a stringer.

"Curtis Poling!" Seeing him was the first good news I'd had all day. Curtis was a charming and slightly bawdy man who lived in the Senior Sunset, a few rooms down from Mrs. Berns. He fished off the roof, so people said he was crazy, but I knew that he was crazy like a fox and twice as cute. He'd helped me crack Jeff's murder case in May. "What're you doing out?"

"I wanted to see about getting my fish mounted, but somehow, I ended up over here." He held up his prize. "She's a beaut, eh?"

I didn't know how attractive she was, but she was big for a sunny, big and stinky. "Catch her off the roof?"

Curtis raised an eyebrow. "You know it. If you find a spot that works, you stick with it."

"You know," I said, "you don't look anything like that fish, Curtis."

"And neither do you, darling. I'd thank you to head me back toward the taxidermy shop, and I'll be on my way." His smile crinkled his ice-blue eyes, still sharp as hooks even though he was pushing ninety.

"You got it. Just let me finish up with this contest."

Kennie had moved on quickly when she'd spotted the dead fish, and when I caught up with her, we agreed that Kasey the retriever and her owner, Brian, were the winners. For their efforts, they received a twenty-five-dollar gift certificate to Scooby's Doo, the local pet-grooming parlor. I thanked everyone for participating, took Curtis by the elbow, and led him back to the Sunset, making a quick detour to the taxidermy shop on our way.

Once I knew Curtis was safely tucked away, I returned to Gina's to retrieve my car and then headed home, forcibly keeping negative thoughts out of my head. That left me idea-free. The lush hardwoods along County Road 83 looked tropical, but there were still no birds singing. The silence made the heat seem even more pregnant, and I wondered when it was going to break. I added "swim in the lake" to my mental list of cleansing activities for this afternoon.

At least Luna was happy to see me, pumping happily up the driveway when she heard my car. Back at the house, I promised ice water and a cool dip in the lake if she'd let me change into my bikini and slap on some sunscreen. Tiger Pop feigned disinterest, but she followed us as we made our way down the tree-shaded lane to our tiny private beach on Whiskey Lake. I could hear families splashing at Shangri-La, the charming resort with a storied past, at the other end of the isthmus.

I tossed my towel to the ground and kept to the grass alongside the mini beach, avoiding the pile of brown sugar sand the local 4H club had delivered before Memorial Day weekend. The sand, I knew from painful experience, would be glassmaking hot this time of day. Sunlight shimmered off the smooth surface of the lake, so bright I couldn't look straight at it. Head down, I walked into the heavenly cool water until I was knee deep and took the plunge. I was never one to acclimate myself slowly. I twisted underwater, my body heat dropping agreeably.

My hands played along the silty bottom of the lake and dragged through the plant life. If I were wearing my diving mask, I'd be able to see silvery fish dart away. As I swam, the image of that dead white foot in Johnny's cabin kept sliding into my brain, leaving an empty feeling inside me. Suddenly, I didn't feel like being in this cold lake anymore.

I pushed myself to the surface. Luna whined at me from the shore. "Come on, you big baby!"

She barked and paddled out toward me. I knew she might scratch me if she got too near, so I swam toward shore, where I found a piece of driftwood and played fetch with her in two feet of water. When she was exhausted and the cooling water had leached the red from my skin, I headed back to the house, not bothering to towel off. Luna and Tiger Pop trailed behind, my sweet little farm groupies.

I was grateful for their steadying presence.

The part of the garden I hadn't worked over on Friday night had reached the Extreme Weeding stage. The plants were *Land of the Lost* massive, and the weeds had stopped seeding weeks ago. If I gave it a good going-over today and used the dead weeds as mulch, I'd have to do only occasional, light weeding for the rest of the summer.

I picked up where I'd left off and dug my fingers into the earth, enjoying the cool feel under the surface. I started at the outer perimeter of the broccoli, cauliflower, and brussels sprout cans. By the time I reached the peas, my rhythm was down to a science. I didn't even stop to snack on the juicy pods. Next it was carrots, then beans, eggplant, squash, and pumpkins, and finally, more marigolds and zinnias. I knew I'd be flush with zinnias by the first blush of August.

By the time I reached the final row, the weeds I'd laid flat at the first were turning a dried, pale green, serving as a warning for all future trespassers. They'd also keep the roots of my vegetables cooler during the scorching July days. For good measure, I raked up two piles of drying grass from my earlier lawn mowing and scattered an extra layer of mulch over the weeds.

When finished, hands on hips, crusty dirt caked to my knees and under my fingernails, I studied my work. The garden was food and comfort in one small, thriving space.

I stretched and studied the position of the sun. I needed to check the birdseed level in my feeders and set out the sprinkler to wet the thirsty garden before I went inside to make supper. I was leaning into the five-gallon metal birdseed bucket when I heard a car crunching up my driveway. I figured it was just some guest heading to Shangri-La and continued my work.

I had a big scoop of seed in hand when the vehicle pulled into my driveway. My stomach clenched when I realized it belonged to Kennie Rogers. I dropped down to my knees when I saw who was sitting next to her.

Chapter 28

Bad Brad, the man I'd loved until he cheated on me (thank god), was not only still in Battle Lake but *at Kennie's side*, wearing a snap-front lab coat covered in a skull-and-crossbones pattern. He wore scruffy Doc Marten boots and carried what looked like a doctor's house-call bag.

I might have whimpered.

"Aren't we lucky to catch you at home, Miss Mira!" Kennie called out as the two of them walked toward me.

I was frozen, gripping a scoop of thistle seed like it was the key to The Door Out. Kennie had warned me that she was coming over later, and what a fool I was for not believing her.

"Brad, I do declare, we're just in time for a Beaver Pelt intervention, wouldn't you say?" Kennie continued. "If ever a girl needed to feel pretty, that girl was Mira." The white lab coat she was wearing over knee-high pleather go-go boots did nothing to relax my stance.

"Now, don't look so scared. My assistant and I are here to save you," she trilled, "if you're ready to be saved."

I for sure wasn't.

I dropped the scoop into the metal bucket and started backing toward the house. It was a flimsy double-wide, so this little pig didn't have much protection, but my only other option was my car, and Dr. Moreau and Mr. Hyde stood between me and it.

"Saved sounds great!" I said. "Let me just go get cleaned up real quick, and we can get on with that."

Brad and Kennie continued advancing, smiling encouragingly. "But that's why we're here. To clean you up, doll!"

My plan was to slip inside the house, lock the front door, and if they tried to break in and have their most certainly unlicensed "Beaver Pelt intervention" way with me, I'd sneak out the back and race to my car. And then I would drive as far from Battle Lake as I could possibly travel on one tank of gas while wearing a bikini.

"Can I at least wash my hands?" I asked.

"No need, sweetie. We have gloves, and we do all the handling. You just lay there!"

I squealed and tripped over my own feet, landing on the soft grass in an ungainly heap.

Brad leaned down and offered me his hand, his mouth pursed in confusion. "Jeez. It's no big deal. Kennie's just running a home-visit cosmopologist service."

"Cosmetologist, hon," Kennie corrected, patting him on the back, "but my specialty is waxing. Eyebrows, mustaches, down below. I got the inspiration from the Beaver Pelts cheerleading squad. Those short skirts, all those old legs in the air." She shuddered. "A Beaver Pelt intervention is a waist-to-big-toe waxing, all for one low price."

I blinked, noisily, and scrambled to my feet without Brad's help. "You came here to give me a bikini wax? With *a guy*?"

She planted her hands on her hips. "I assure you I'm a professional. It's been a decade or so since I took the classes, but I've kept current through a correspondence program."

"What about him?" I was suddenly self-conscious in my swimsuit and drew my thighs together in a slow and controlled movement, so as not to draw attention to my "down below." "What's he doing here?"

Brad smiled serenely. "I have you to thank for that, Mira. I was gonna head back to the Cities with the band after the show, but you just looked so happy when I ran into you. I wanted to see if small-town life would work for me, too."

Kennie glanced from Brad to me, a cross between crabby and curious. "Wait. You two know each other?"

"Not anymore," I said.

"And not like I know you, right, hon?" Kennie winked at Brad.

Brad smiled at her but spoke to me. "When Kennie came by to pay us after our gig, she said I could crash at her place until I got settled."

That's when I noticed Brad's legs were hairless.

I turned off my brain before the picture went any farther north, but dang if karma wasn't dealing me a confusing hand. My cheating ex was in town, but he appeared to be facing his own punishment at the hand of a wild waxer. I couldn't process it. What I needed was a shower, supper, and a little bland television. "I appreciate you driving out here, Kennie, but I don't get waxed."

"There's a first time for everything."

I shook my head. "Not true."

She pouted. "I'll give you a 50 percent discount."

"Kennie, I'm not going to pay you to rip my hair out with hot wax."

"I have to help you out somehow, sweets." She raised her penciled-in eyebrows hopefully. "How about a teeny tiny little makeover?"

She obviously wasn't going to leave without touching me. "How teeny tiny?"

"Just a little mascara and a dust of lip gloss," she said, clapping her hands happily. "It'll brighten your pretty eyes right up. They're all deep set now, like two holes drilled into your skull."

I sighed. If she had to go after something, my face seemed like the safest bet. I wasn't going to let them in my house, though. I rinsed off as best I could with the garden hose and set myself on the front porch steps, hands on knees. Brad opened up his doctor's bag to reveal a pot of wax, strips of paper, evil-looking four-inch tweezers, a comb, a brush, scissors, hair spray, and a full palette makeup kit. He pulled out the kit and held it open for Kennie, who studied me disapprovingly.

"You're tanned as brown as a bean farmer."

"Sorry."

"You're going to look like raisin leather before you're forty, you know that?" she scolded. "And you have field-worker hands."

I groaned. "Just do the makeup, OK? I haven't eaten supper yet."

Kennie sniffed and huffed but didn't say anything else as she began applying makeup. This close to her face, I could see the putty-knife precision she used to get herself through the day. There was a bronze makeup lip around the perimeter of her face, and her glitter eye shadow was thick and unblended. Her lips were an unflattering apricot shade. Sigh. At least I was home, and I could wash off whatever damage she did.

Brad tried to make supportive "oohing" sounds throughout the process, but his eyes kept getting wider and wider as I felt myself buried under Kennie's fall colors. Even Luna and Tiger Pop were watching now.

Twenty long minutes later, Kennie pronounced herself done. "That is what they call a make*over*. Brad, hand me the mirror."

I thought of the "Mira Mira" song he'd recently sung to me. "No Mira. I mean, no mirror." I wanted them out of here. "I'm sure it looks fabulous. How much do I owe you?"

Kennie chuckled. "Honey, consider me your drug dealer. The first one's free. Once you're hooked, we talk prices. Now don't waste that pretty face at home. You should come to town tonight and show yourself off."

I smiled at the unlikeliness of that happening. "Good idea. I suppose you two need to go drum up more business, eh?"

"You know the life of the working woman too well! No rest for the wicked. You know where to find me." She twittered her fingers at me and herded Brad away before he'd fully closed his doctor's bag.

I was not sorry to see them go. I made a mental note to start carrying my stun gun around with me, even when wearing a bikini. I went inside to wash my face in a cool shower. I was locking the door behind me—I hadn't totally ruled out Kennie resorting to a forcible bikini wax—when the phone rang. I didn't bother to check the caller ID, that's how much of a hurry I was in to wash my face.

"Hello?"

"Mira? It's Johnny."

Chapter 29

My heart thudded on a crest of mixed feelings. "Where are you?"

"I'm still in Stevens Point. In Wisconsin."

My voice took on an edge. "And how's your grandma?"

I heard a deep sigh through the crackling of the phone line. Johnny must have been calling on his cell. "I'm sorry, Mira. I never went to see my grandma. I lied to you."

More confusion. "Why?"

"I needed you to watch my cabin, and if I told you where I was really going, I wasn't sure you'd do it."

Score one for my theory that he was hooking up with Dolly. "So where'd you really go?"

There was another crackle on the line. ". . . Stevens Point. Dolly teaches here, at the University of . . ."

He faded out, but I'd heard enough. I almost hung up when his voice ghosted back over the line. "She vandalized a McDonald's."

"What? You're cutting out."

"Hold on." There was a little more static, and then his voice came through clear as crystal. "I came to Stevens Point to find out what I could about Dolly Castle. Last night at the fireworks? I was trying to find out where she teaches. I think she's behind Chief Wenonga's disappearance. I wanted to come here to see what I could find out."

My heart warmed a crack. Was it possible Johnny was just as interested in getting the Chief back as I was, and had a legitimate reason to lie and hang out with Dolly? "And you found out she vandalized a McDonald's?"

"Not the building, the Ronald McDonald statues in front of the restaurants. In India. Apparently, she was over there for study abroad in some place called Shatrunjaya Hills, and her group went activist and spray-painted messages on the Ronald McDonalds, chopped off limbs, added horns. Dolly was arrested and extradited to the United States. She ended up paying a hefty fine."

"So what does that tell us?" I asked impatiently.

"I don't know. That she knows how to mess with fiberglass? That she's not afraid of breaking the law?" He was quiet for a beat. "You sound mad. I thought you would think this was good news."

My thawing heart ached. Johnny really did sound like he wanted to impress me. The one critical point he'd failed to address was the dead body in the cabin he'd asked me to watch for him. "Is there anything else you called about?"

"... can't hear you ..."

"IS THERE ANYTHING ELSE YOU WANT TO TELL ME?"

"... reception ... of nowhere ..."

"THERE IS A DEAD BODY IN YOUR CABIN. DO YOU WANT TO TALK ABOUT IT?"

"... body in my dad's cabin? What are you talking about?"

I lowered my voice to normal range. "The police found a dead body in your cabin today. Now they're looking for you. Whose body is it?" The other end of the line was absolutely quiet. "Johnny? Whose body is it?"

His voice came out hushed, and it wasn't the connection. "I have no idea."

"Don't lie to me again." Tears stung my eyes. *Please.*

"I have no idea whose body it is." He sounded husky, worried. "I'm on my way back. I'll go straight to the police station and ..."

There was a snap on the line, and it went dead. I held it to my ear for several seconds longer, and then hit the "End" button on my phone. My caller ID registered only an "Unknown Name, Unknown Number."

I plopped onto my couch, thoughts ricocheting, wishing I'd brought Gina's bottle of vodka home with me.

Chapter 30

I squared my shoulders. As much as I wanted to believe Johnny hadn't really been hooking up with Dolly and knew nothing about the dead guy, I wasn't going to let myself be played for the fool again. I tried to shove pictures of Johnny out of my head, but in the sultry heat of my living room, I couldn't escape the memory of him smiling at me as he helped me garden in June, or the image of his strong hands digging into freshly turned dirt, or even his sweetly shy smile as he dropped me off after supper last night. These hot thoughts pulsed through my mind as a mosquito whined around my head. I slapped at it and missed.

It was soon joined by a second. Then another.

I checked my front door, and it was locked tight. I couldn't find a hole in any of the screens, either. I fixed myself a cold cheese-and-pickle sandwich and scarfed it down. I rinsed the plate, stacked it in the sink, and made myself a glass of ice water. The glass fogged up immediately, and drips of water glided down the sides and over my fingers. I should definitely shower, but I was suddenly so exhausted I could hardly stand up. It'd been a day. I figured it'd be easier to wash my sheets tomorrow than myself tonight. Unfortunately, by now more mosquitoes had joined the first ones, their telltale humming promising a miserable night.

I tried to outrun them by dashing into my bedroom and slamming the door. I set the sweating water glass next to my bed and flopped down, a fan pointed on my body. I wanted to think, but whenever the breeze from the oscillating fan moved from my head, the mosquitoes returned, buzzing and keening with a vengeance. It sounded like a bona fide swarm, but as soon as I killed one, two more appeared. When I pointed the fan so it was aimed at only my face, one of them bit my ankle and escaped scot-free.

Frustrated, I tried lying under the sheets, but I could still hear their whining. They were hovering, just waiting for me to relax and expose my vulnerable skin. I tossed and turned and wondered what Gary Wohnt would do to Johnny. Throw him into the county jail in Fergus Falls, certainly, and how would they treat him there?

I was bitten again, this time on the tender flesh of my wrist, and I jumped out of bed and returned to the couch. The drone of the mosquitoes was driving me crazy. I couldn't think a clear thought and I certainly couldn't sleep between the heavy heat and the bloodthirsty flying knives invading my home. My choices were to either stay here and lose my mind or drive into town and see if the Battle Lake Motel had a vacancy. I could fix whatever chink in my double-wide armor they were coming through tomorrow, in the light of day.

Before I started to fret about the money I'd be wasting, I scooped up a toothbrush, a change of clothes, and a hairbrush. On my way out, I made sure Tiger Pop and Luna's door worked and that they had plenty of food and water. I could still hear the whining insects as I got in my car, so I rolled down all the windows and sped down County Road 83. Only when I finally reached the outskirts of Battle Lake did I feel bug-free.

When I pulled into the motel parking lot, I spotted Dolly's black Honda and, a few cars down, Brando's red Hummer. I scratched absentmindedly at the itchy welts across my arms. When I'd questioned Les at his shop after Randy Myers disappeared, he mentioned that Brando was staying in a cabin north of town, but I had no reason to trust Les. Brando could be staying at the motel, or maybe he was visiting Dolly, confirming my earlier hunch that the two of them knew each other. Was the motel his destination when he'd first tailgated me?

A little window peeking was clearly in order, but first, I needed to stop by and visit Chief Wenonga's pedestal to see if there was anything new on the scene, or something that both the police and I had overlooked. Heat lightning flashed across the glass-flat surface of Battle Lake as I stepped out of my car, making chills race across my arms. A storm in this heat would be fierce.

I sniffed the air for ozone but smelled only lake and country. I reached back into my car for my flashlight and headed to Wenonga's former digs. The half-full moon offered enough illumination that I didn't click on my light as I walked, listening to the tinkle of glass and muted laughter floating across the lake.

The base was just as I'd left it two days and a million years ago, minus the blood. The four posts had been scrubbed clean and pointed angrily toward the night sky. They were cool to the touch, as was the four-foot-high concrete pedestal.

Clicking on my flashlight revealed nothing new. The grass perimeter was also scrubbed clean—not even a cigarette butt marred the trampled lawn. Remembering how debris-free (minus the scalp) the area had also been on Friday when I first discovered Wenonga missing gave me pause. If the Chief-stealer had used a wrecking ball, as Brando had said they'd need to, there would have been shrapnel everywhere. Instead, the ground had been as clean as a hospital floor.

I got on my knees and ran my fingers through the stubbly grass to make sure I wasn't missing something.

"What're you doing?"

The gruff voice made me jump up so fast that I dropped my flashlight, and it clicked itself off as it landed. I couldn't make out anyone in the light of the half moon.

"Who said that?"

"I am the night. I am swift justice. I am—"

I sighed. "Les, is that you?"

He shuffled out from behind a tree, a set of night-vision goggles perched on his head. I reached down for my flashlight; clicked it back on, sending a wild strip of light down the park; and shined it on Les. He was dressed head to toe in Realtree camo with grease paint smeared across his cheeks.

"What're you doing out here late at night?" he asked.

"I could ask you the same thing."

"I'm hunting," he said defensively.

I didn't think there was anything in season, not in town. "For what?"

He held my gaze. "The truth."

I laughed. I couldn't help myself. "I guess I am, too. You find any?"

"Not yet, but I just started." The front office door to the Battle Lake Motel opened, spilling a rectangle of yellow light into the parking lot. Someone stepped out, their voice carrying across the distance. Les hit the ground and pulled me with him. "Get down!"

I fell with an audible *whomp*, my bones rattled. "You wouldn't happen to be searching for this truth at the Battle Lake Motel, would you?" I said when I caught my breath.

"Maybe," he said evasively.

A thought struck me. "You said Brando is staying at a cabin north of town?"

His nostrils flared. "What of it?" he asked.

"So what's his Hummer doing at the motel?"

Les broke off eye contact. The motel door closed, and we both stood up, brushing the dirt off our knees.

"Les?"

"Could be he's visiting someone."

I decided to approach this from another angle. "Say, how would you take down the Chief Wenonga statue if you had to do it?"

He eyed me suspiciously. "I didn't steal the statue."

I sighed. "Look, I saw you following Dolly at the fireworks, and now you're spying on her outside her motel room. If I tell Gary Wohnt what you're up to, you're going to have an uncomfortable lot of surveillance in your life. How about you cooperate with me now, and I'll keep quiet about your illicit activities?"

He started to puff up, his bowling-ball face glistening under the blackness, and then, just as quickly, he deflated. "I'm just guessing, you understand? I didn't take that statue, but if I did, I'd take it down with a blowtorch and a cherry picker, lickety-split. No mess, and you could get it done in under forty-five minutes. That's just a guess, mind you."

I processed that, wondering why Brando had lied. Or maybe he really had no idea how to dismantle a fiberglass statue? "What were you talking to Brando about the other night, when he stormed out of your store?"

Les kicked at the dirt. "I knew he was coming to town. I overheard Kennie and Gary talking about it one night when I was strolling past Kennie's house. I arranged a visit with Brando, thinking I could talk him into making a big white-guy statue for Battle Lake."

I'd *bet* he was just strolling past Kennie's house. I wondered who else's house he strolled past regularly. "What did Brando say?"

"He didn't think it would be a good idea." He tipped his head thoughtfully. "Say, you look awful pretty tonight."

The incongruousness of his statement made it hard to process. "What?"

Another door opened in the Battle Lake Motel, but this time, it wasn't the office. It was number 7—Dolly Castle's—and a victorious-looking Brando was strutting through it. Both Les and I held our breath, and I had to stifle a yelp when Dolly's strawberry-blonde head peeked out and kissed Brando passionately before she slapped him on the rear and closed the door behind him.

They sure *did* know each other.

"How long have they been messing around?" I looked away from the rumbling Hummer. "Les?" He was gone, like a mole underground. I sighed and stood, dragging my exhausted bones back to the motel. I needed some sleep before I collapsed. I'd just spent the last of my fumes dealing with Les.

I entered the motel office and dinged the bell at the front desk. I heard a cheerful voice warble from the back room. "I'm on my way! It's a busy night here at the Battle Lake Motel. We have just one room . . . oh my!"

The face of the middle-aged desk clerk went from welcoming to surprised to suspicious. I glanced over my shoulder—no one behind me—and back at her, smiling uncertainly. "Um, were you saying you have one room left?"

"We're a family hotel."

"Oh, it's just me tonight." I smiled with more confidence.

"We are a *family* motel." Her lips pursed so tightly they nearly disappeared. "We don't need your kind's business."

I stared around the front office, trying to find some indication of what my kind was versus what kind they were accepting. That's when I caught my reflection off the glass of the 5 x 7, framed Ducks Unlimited print over the front desk. I still wore all the makeup that Kennie had slathered on me earlier, and it did not look pretty.

That was, unless one was in the market for a ten-dollar prostitute.

"Jesus," I whispered.

"It's a little late for him, don't you think?"

"No. I mean yes!" I shook my head furiously. "I mean, I'm not what you think I am. I, um, let my five-year-old niece put makeup on me earlier tonight and must have forgotten to wash it off. My name is Mira James. I run the library and work at the newspaper."

Her lips stayed as tight as a razor cut across her face. "And why do you need a room if you live in town, Ms. James?"

"I don't live in town. I live west of town, at Sunny Waters's place?" I knew I was stressed because I hardly ever referred to the double-wide as Sunny's anymore. "There's a hole in one of the screens, but I couldn't find where, and my bedroom was swarming with mosquitoes. I needed to get a good night's sleep. OK?"

Her lips relaxed only marginally. "I need to see some ID."

Thankfully, my new driver's license had arrived in the mail the week before. Heaven help me if I'd handed her something with a Minneapolis address. I offered her my ID. "See? I live west of town."

She examined the plastic card much longer than necessary before snapping it on the counter and sliding it toward me. "I hope I don't see any male companionship entering your room tonight, Ms. James. It would be a shame if I had to call Battle Lake police chief Gary Wohnt out here to interrupt your, *ahem*, activities."

I snorted at the image of Gary receiving that phone call. "You don't need to worry. How much is the room?"

"Fifty-five dollars plus tax."

"Gotcha." I handed her cash and took my room key. Lucky number 8, right next to Dolly, who was doing just fine for male companionship, thank you very much. I bet *she* hadn't gotten the hairy eyeball from the desk clerk.

I grabbed the small bundle of toiletries from my car and headed toward my room, grateful at the prospect of a night in air-conditioned comfort. There was one last hunch I needed to follow up on before I retired for the night, though.

I stopped at Dolly's car, my flashlight in my hands, and tried to look underneath while keeping my tender knees off the gravel. In the moonlight, I didn't see anything but mud spatter, but when I ran my hands over it and it didn't flake off, I shined my light and peered closer.

Sure enough—dried red paint was splattered on her undercarriage. I felt a surge of triumph, followed by horror.

Dr. Dolly had done some four-wheeling out at Johnny's cabin.

Had she also left a dead body there?

Chapter 31

In the air-conditioned, mosquito-free, blackout-dark motel, I slept like a tranq-darted rhino. I woke up feeling refreshed, distanced from the corpse I'd seen, capable, like I could solve all this and bring Chief Wenonga home. After witnessing Brando leave Dolly's room, and then discovering the red paint on her car, it was plain as the mosquito bites on my ankle that they were my bad guys. I just had to figure out how and why.

After I finished my library shift, I'd drive out to Johnny's cabin to see if I'd missed anything, and then I'd enlist Gary Wohnt's help to get Johnny off the hook. Together, we'd find out why the Chief had been snatched, how it was connected to Randy Myers's disappearance, and how that all related to the dead guy in Johnny's cabin. I showered, brushed my teeth, and checked out of the motel.

The town of Battle Lake was beautiful and humming, the lake skirting the north edge of town sparkling in the sunlight. I decided to leave my vehicle in the motel lot near Dolly's and walk the twenty minutes to work. It felt good to be heading back to the library, where there was some order.

While we were past the Fourth of July, tourists would be packing the town all week. Families in brightly colored sundresses and T-shirts walked the streets, stopping at the apothecary for sunscreen and mosquito repellent, window-shopping at the local stores that wouldn't open for another hour.

I felt good enough to treat myself to iced green tea and a bagel at the Fortune Café. The coffee shop was packed. I waited my turn and was greeted by Sid's smiling face.

"You look like the cat who got the mouse," she said, her cheaters pushed on top of her head. Her eyes crinkled beautifully at the corners.

"I hope to be the chick who gets the statue," I replied, salivating as I studied the baked goods in the case. "You heard about the dead body at Johnny's cabin?"

She studied me. "Just that it was scalped. Please tell me you weren't the one who found it."

I made a zipper motion across my mouth.

"Shoot," she said. "If it wasn't for bad luck . . . You OK?"

I nodded, blinking back the sudden heat in my eyes. As long as no one offered me sympathy, I could skate on the surface of it. "I'm fine."

She read me for a few seconds. Just when I was sure she was going to offer me a hug—which would shut me down emotionally for at least a week, if not permanently—she sighed, as if making up her mind to honor my need to compartmentalize no matter how much she wished it were different. "Can I get you some iced tea?"

"Please, green sweetened. And an everything bagel with olive cream cheese, to go." I glanced around at the crowd filling her shop. "Your business seems to be doing fine."

She scooped a pile of ice into a disposable cup. "Most of these people just arrived. If word spreads that it's not safe in Battle Lake, I don't know what's going to happen. The only good news is that the dead guy isn't local."

"That's not good news to an out-of-towner, I suppose." I made a face and traded my cash for the bagel and tea. Threading my way through the crowd and out the door, I wondered what sort of tourists Battle Lake would start drawing if this murder wasn't solved soon. It'd be awful. A lot of people I cared about had their incomes tied to Battle Lake. That gave me one more reason to solve the murder.

The library was just as I'd left it, and the air-conditioned oxygen felt refreshing against my face. I tossed my keys on the front counter, eyeballed the stack of books in the drop box that needed shelving, and whistled as I headed to the back room to check my messages.

It might have been the start of a perfect day if not for the man in my rear office, buck naked but for a faux Native American headdress and some war paint.

Chapter 32

I'm not ashamed to say I screamed, and for the second time in under a week. At the sound of my shriek, the man jumped behind my desk and crouched down, his face redder than the paint streaked across his chest.

I darted forward to grab the stapler off my desk and lunged back, wielding the implement staples out. "Who are you?"

He held his hands in front of him in the universal sign of "don't hurt me, this is a big misunderstanding." That's when Mrs. Berns strutted out from the bathroom. Her blouse was unbuttoned down the front, revealing a puckered bra, and her hair was disheveled. Around her waist, she had a gun belt strung low, cap-shooters stuck in each of the holsters. That's when I noticed the mess—candy bar wrappers, empty water and wine bottles, microwaved food containers piled in the trash, a tube of something I was too uncomfortable to examine closely on the edge of my desk.

Mrs. Berns appeared annoyed to see me. "It's Sunday. Even God rested on Sunday. Don't you have any social life?"

My glance spun from the naked-but-for-headwear guy crouched behind my desk to Mrs. Berns, and back again to the nude guy. "It's Monday, Mrs. Berns."

"Monday?" She hooted and slapped her leg. "Well, put a hitch in my giddy-up! We've been playing for two whole days, Randy! No wonder I was so hungry."

As the hangdog man scrambled to gather loose paper off my desk to cover his pork and beans, realization began to dawn. "*Randy?* Not Randy Myers, by any chance?"

He nodded, clutching an invoice across his privates, and sheepishly offered me his free hand. "None other. Sorry for the scare."

I have a rule against shaking hands with naked men, one that I have to invoke more often than you'd think. I ground my fists into my hips. "Do you know the *whole town* is looking for you? They thought you were kidnapped."

Mrs. Berns pulled out a gun and let a sulfurous pop into the air, cackling. "He was! I got him!"

A ridiculous thought dawned on me. "Mrs. Berns, you didn't take the big Indian, too, did you?"

She tipped her head. "They come in different sizes?"

"I meant Chief Wenonga."

"Hell no, girl." She cackled. "What would I do with a big fiberglass statue? Randy here is all the man I need. It's all in the name."

"No shit?" he said, a pleased smile lighting up his face.

"Not even a little turd."

I released a breath. There was one crime solved: Mrs. Berns had absconded with poor Randy Myers and had been having her way with him since Saturday. "I'm glad you two were enjoying yourselves, but Randy better get some clothes on and tell Gary Wohnt that he's all right." I wrinkled my nose at the mess. "And I wouldn't hate it if you kept the library out of your love life in the future."

She showed zero shame. "My tax dollars pay for this library, too, little missy, so as long as I have a library card, I will use it as I please."

I knew Mrs. Berns possessed keys to nearly every business in Battle Lake (thanks mostly to a bad habit of stealing the spares), so there was no point in arguing. "Can you two just take it elsewhere? I need to open up in forty-five minutes."

"Fine." She made a hand motion to Randy, indicating he should get dressed. "I'll be back around lunchtime to help you with the tourist rush."

"Thank you." I turned to leave them to their cleanup.

"Wait!" Mrs. Berns said. "Have I missed any new obituaries in the last coupla days? Folks at the Sunset get mad if I don't tell them who died and they have to find out from the newspaper."

"No new obits that I've heard." I didn't tell her about the guy in the cabin. No need to worry her until he'd been identified.

She appeared thoughtful as she buttoned up the front of her blouse. "You know how I'd like to go? One of those stuttering strokes. A little notice and then you're gone. That's what Lydia Thorfinnson had, that lucky old coot."

My heart unexpectedly warmed. Mrs. Berns was one of a kind. I was lucky to know her, even if she had trashed my office. "If you ever do die, I'm sure you'll do it with style."

That seemed to satisfy her. She began clearing surfaces while Randy skedaddled into the bathroom. I returned to the main room and kept busy shelving books and watering plants, careful not to make eye contact when the two left, though I noticed he looked a little saddle sore as he limped toward the door. Mrs. Berns seemed none the worse for wear.

As soon as I had the library ready for business, I planted myself at the front computer. I needed to send 1,500 words to Ron Sims today, and he wanted it in three articles. The first piece would summarize the mundane parts of Wenonga Days. The second would be the Mira's Musings column I'd already started, but what would the third article be about? I figured it would be best to start writing and see what came. First, the Wenonga Days straight stuff.

Annual Wenonga Days Festival Well Attended

This year, Wenonga Days started with a bang. Although the Chief missed his own celebration, he was there in spirit throughout the weekend. Crazy Days on Friday brought in a crowd of people shopping for bargains as every business on Lake Street offered discounts from 25 to 75 percent off original prices.

Friday evening, an estimated 400 people attended the street dance to hear Not with My Horse, a Minneapolis band, serenade the crowd with their unique country-punk fusion. The Rusty Nail sponsored the dance.

For those who were up early Saturday, the Battle Lake Jaycees offered a Kiddie Karnival and Turtle Races. Ashley Grosbain's turtle was the clear winner at the races. The parade that followed featured marching bands from all over Minnesota, Dalton's Antique Thresher review, and as a special surprise, Mayor Kennie Rogers and her group of radical cheerleaders, calling themselves "The Beaver Pelts," shared their moves with the crowd.

Also present at the parade was Brando Erikkson, owner of the fiberglass company Fibertastic Enterprises, which created Chief Wenonga. At the parade, Mr. Erikkson offered to donate a slightly irregular fiberglass woodchuck to replace the Wenonga statue.

The woodchuck will be delivered to Halverson Park early this week.

The Saturday night fireworks, made possible due to the annual fundraiser sponsored by the Battle Lake

Chamber of Commerce, were a big hit with families who viewed them from Glendalough Park. The display cost nearly $20,000 and lasted 25 minutes. There were no reported injuries.

The winner of Sunday's 30K bike race in the female category was Linda Clarkson; the winner in the male category was Erik Schultz. Nikki Welde was the winner of the 5K run in the female category; Jerome Teske was the winner in the male category.

There was a grand turnout for the Pet and Owner Look-Alike Contest, but only one pair could win. This year, that lucky duo was Brian Green of Urbank and Kasey, his golden retriever.

The all-town garage sale offered a backdrop to Sunday's races. From start to finish, it's going to be hard to top this year's Wenonga Days.

I hit "Save" and sat back in my captain's chair. Writing the first article hadn't been too hard; sending it with the photos I'd snapped would create a great overview of the weekend. Now it was time to write the piece about the missing Chief. I built off my earlier draft, deleting the paragraph I'd written about Randolph Myers, seeing as how he'd most definitely been found.

It's My Party, and I'll Fly if I Want To

In a strange turn of events, Chief Wenonga disappeared from Battle Lake on Friday, July 3, just as the plans for his 20th birthday party were finalized. Police on the scene Friday morning found only four anchoring posts at the statue's base and what appeared to be blood at the Halverson Park location where the Chief had stood proudly for two decades.

Battle Lake was named for a melee between the Ojibwe—including the real-life Wenonga—and Dakota that took place more than 200 years ago. The Ojibwe, led by Chief Ukkewaus, gathered nearly 50 warriors to stage what they believed was a surprise attack. However, the Dakota were prepared, and many Ojibwe died. Wenonga led the surviving warriors back to Leech Lake, where he lived to an old age and was greatly respected by his tribe. The Battle Lake Civic and Commerce Club ordered the Wenonga statue in 1979 and initially placed it in another section of Battle Lake. The Chief was moved to Halverson Park in 1986, where he stood until his disappearance last Friday.

In what appears to be a connected case, the body of an unidentified male was found in a cabin north of Battle Lake on Saturday evening. Battle Lake Police are calling this case a homicide and are currently following up on several leads.

Battle Lake has recently been the site of several strange occurrences, including the murder of Battle Lake alumnus Jeff Wilson in May. That mystery was solved shortly after, and it is the hope of the people of Battle Lake that this latest case will be cracked soon also, so the normally safe and peaceful town can resume life as usual.

I didn't know if "resume" was an accurate word to use in the final paragraph, but I was too busy dealing with the hot slice of pain that came with typing Jeff's name to change it. I'd been falling head to toe in love with him, and he was gone forever. *Me and men.* Maybe I could hire myself out to women who'd been dumped by or couldn't get rid of cheaters, abusers, emotional withholders, and, of course, the foreplay challenged. After their mistreating man had a few dates with me, the problem would be solved.

I'd call it the Jinx Man-Away Service, and Kennie Rogers could be my manager. Come to think of it, maybe Mrs. Berns could get involved, too.

I flicked my cheek to turn off the inner negative-talk and refocused on my computer. I had two articles down and one more to write, and I had no blessed idea what it was going to be about. I sipped at my aromatic jasmine tea and felt inspiration glide down my throat.

Battle Lake Has Beauty and Backbone

The village of Battle Lake officially came into existence Halloween 1881, when it was platted for Torger O. and Bertie O. Holdt. By 1885, there were 182 residents, but newspaper references at the time allude to unusual amounts of bad luck being visited on the inhabitants—mysterious plagues, crop rot, and intense weather were only the beginning.

The first white settlers found Native American mounds scattered in the region, 42 near the lake's inlet alone. Local legend had it that whoever took over the land that had once belonged to the Indians would be cursed. In the last few months, it is hard to ignore the specter of a curse as the town has contended with three murders in as many months—Jeff Wilson found dead in the library in May, a carnival gone horribly awry in June, and now the missing Chief Wenonga statue and homicide in July.

Although it would be easy to write Battle Lake off as cursed, it'd be a mistake. The town offers relaxation and warm smiles to visitors year-round and is a full-service town with a dentist, chiropractor, and clinic, as well as the Village Apothecary available to meet the sundry and pharmaceutical needs of locals and tourists alike. The town's excellent newspaper keeps readers apprised of local happenings.

Battle Lake also has unique stores for window-shopping or finding that special present, from the Bramble and the Rose to O'kay Gifts. Granny's Pantry sells ice cream cones bigger than your head and old-fashioned candy by the basket, and the Fortune Café makes the best homemade ginger scones in the county.

If you're one of the few not lucky enough to catch sunnies and trophy walleyes for supper, delicious food is easy to find in Battle Lake, from the eggs Benedict at the Shoreline to the Tater Tot hotdish at the Turtle Stew to the butter knife steaks and fresh-baked bread at Stub's.

If you're only in town for a brief stay, there are more than 30 safe, clean, and fun places to stay, from Shangri-La to the Battle Lake Motel to the Last Resort. If you're in town for longer, the streets are safe, the schools are good, and the community is united. Battle Lake may have gotten a rough start and had its share of misfortunes, but the town remains strong in the face of it all.

Battle Lake is, after all, easy to get to and hard to leave.

I winced at my last sentence—it *was* hard to leave a place when you were dead—but I felt good about the article. A lot of salt-of-the-earth people were working and running businesses in town, and they shouldn't be punished just because a few murderers had found their way here. I saved all three pieces and emailed them as attachments along with their accompanying photos, just as the phone rang.

"James, where are my articles?"

"Hi, Ron. It's not noon yet. That was my deadline."

He was quiet for a beat. "Deadlines are for the weak and undisciplined."

Then why bother giving them? "The articles are hurtling through cyberspace and into your computer as we speak," I said smugly. "Maybe I should get a raise?"

"Maybe you should locate me a new recipe for next week's paper. People can't get enough of that garbage you find. I don't know how you do it."

"It's a gift." I switched the handset from one ear to the other. "Say, whaddya know about the dead body found out at Johnny's cabin?"

A reluctant grunt traveled through the wire. "Can you keep a secret?" he asked.

Technically, I wouldn't be lying if I said yes. I could *theoretically* keep a secret, even if I might not keep *this* secret. "You know it."

"I *don't* know it, and if you spill this before Wohnt makes it public, you're out one reporting job. The corpse didn't have any ID, but a wallet washed up in Silver Lake. The photo and vital stats on the driver's license found in it seem to match the deceased. His name was Liam Anderson, he was from Wausau, Wisconsin, and that's all I know."

Wausau? Why did that sound familiar? I'd never been, and I didn't think I knew anyone from there. Dolly and Brando were from Stevens Point. It might be worth my time to research how close the two towns were. I still needed to get back out to Johnny's cabin, too, but that would have to wait until I closed the library at six. "Thanks for the tip. I'll keep it close to my chest."

"Just get me a recipe before the end of the week." Ron coughed. "Friday is the end of the week."

The phone went *click*, and I was alone in the library. I went to a computer and opened Rand McNally online. Wausau was 361 miles east of Battle Lake, but Stevens Point was only 34 miles south of Wausau. That was a little too close for comfort.

Could I trust Johnny at his word? He said he'd been in Stevens Point only to dig up dirt on Dolly. The more I thought about it, the more I realized he could have been feeding me a whole zoo full of lyin'. When the library door opened with a *dong*, I glanced up anxiously. In walked a woman and three children, all under the age of ten. I smiled at them and exited the map program.

While they browsed the children's section, I returned to reshelving books. A steady crowd began coming shortly after, and I was so busy answering questions that the morning flew. By the time Mrs. Berns came in at one, I was starving. I chose to ignore the fact that I had only hours earlier seen her at the afterglow stage of a weekend sexcapade.

"Hi, Mrs. Berns. Hope you came ready to work. We're busy today."

She appeared sprightly and innocent, her eyes wide and blue and her apricot hair still in curlers. She was wearing a Shania Twain concert T-shirt, cutoff jean shorts, and orthopedic shoes. She smacked her own butt. "I've been working it since I was born, girl."

"OK. Do you mind if I run and get some lunch?"

"Nope." She tapped her chin thoughtfully. "But I thought you might want to bop over to Fergus Falls instead."

I eyed her suspiciously. She was straightening out the pencils on the front desk. "Why?"

"Oh, because they arrested your boy toy, Johnny Leeson, for murder."

Chapter 33

I felt myself sucked into a hole that started in my own stomach. "What?"

"They found a dead body in his cabin, and they took him in." Mrs. Berns shrugged as she stepped behind the front counter. "I thought maybe you could squeeze in a conjugal visit before they send him on to Folsom."

I couldn't close my mouth.

She scowled. "Don't look so surprised. As soon as you so much as glance sideways at a guy, his life slides into the shitter. You're bad luck ten ways from Sunday."

I stood numb as a statue until the hot tears cracked through. "You're right."

Mrs. Berns stopped straightening the counter and stared at me, disgust written across her face. "What? You're going to give up like that? I am not *right*. I'm just a bitchy old woman." She made a shooing motion. "Go fix this. *Go.* I'll watch the library."

"I don't know, Mrs. Berns. Maybe it'd be better if I—"

"Shut your piehole with the 'I don't know,'" she said, glaring. "You found Jeff's murderer in May, you got rid of that ratty Jason Blunt in June, and now you're going to spring Johnny Leeson." Her grimace dropped as her face lit up. "Let me know if you need help, by the way. I've always wanted to break into a prison."

"But what if he's guilty?" There. I'd said it out loud.

She leaned toward me, fire in her eyes. "I'll tell you this only one time, Mira James. I know you've had a tough life, but you're not the only one, so get over it. If you start chasing shadows and mistrusting everyone, you're going to miss everything good." She poked me, hard, in my chest. "Now, do you honestly think Johnny Leeson murdered someone?"

I blinked once, twice, my mouth still open. After scouring my heart and head, I made room for the possibility that Johnny had been up front with me, except for the lapse when he didn't tell me he was driving to Stevens Point to investigate Dolly. But could I really consider trusting him? I didn't feel good about giving another guy a chance to destroy me. There was bad luck, and then there was just plain stupidity.

I had been too young to be responsible for my dad's death, and I was willing to chalk Jeff up to fickle fate, but the other men in my life hadn't exactly been model partners. There was Bad Brad, of course. The cheater. Before him was Kyle from my hometown, who I'd run into in the Cities and started dating during my sophomore year of college. I'd thought I was in love with him, but he was so afraid of commitment that he wouldn't even make a dinner reservation.

Scattered among my love life wreckage were various bad dates, including but not limited to a guy who peed uphill on the AstroTurf of the fifteenth hole of the golf course on our first date. In his defense, it was a long course.

For mini golf.

No, if I took Johnny's side, and he turned out to be a liar, I wouldn't be able to trust myself again. Unfortunately, my other option was to let him twist in the wind and hope that Wohnt caught the real murderer soon.

Curse words.

I kicked at the carpeting, feeling Mrs. Berns's eyes still on me. Why couldn't I just be one of those chicks whose biggest worry was what shoes went with her cute sundress, and the fifty-two best ways to flirt?

Instead, I had to decide whether to help the hot guy who may or may not be lying to me about the dead body in his dad's cabin.

Double curse words.

I made up my mind. "No, I don't think he killed anyone. But—"

"Shush," Mrs. Berns said, not letting me finish. "That's all you need. Go. Sissy crybaby girl."

I didn't know if she was trying to make me feel better or worse, but she was right that I couldn't stay here and worry about Johnny in jail all day.

I needed to race out to his cabin and see what I could find to fix all this.

Chapter 34

I was infinitely less "Snow White with birds landing on my shoulders" optimistic on my way back to my car in the motel parking lot than I had been leaving it. I took the time to notice that Dolly's Honda was gone and wondered where a woman who was in town only to protest Chief Wenonga Days went once the statue disappeared and the celebration had passed.

I supposed that depended on whether she'd accomplished her mission.

I made my way to Silver Lake and was not surprised at the yellow-and-black police tape streamed across Johnny's driveway. Fortunately, there were no cops in sight, so I parked my car a hundred or so feet from the entrance and hoofed it back.

If I took Johnny out of the mix, my working theory was that Dolly, Brando, and the freshly deceased Liam Anderson had removed Chief Wenonga for some unknown reason that benefited all three. Their deal went sour, and when Liam threatened to turn them in, Dolly and Brando killed him, depositing a chunk of his scalp on the base of the statue as some sort of message. I knew Johnny had been to his cabin Saturday afternoon to set up the balloons, so Dolly and Brando must have stashed the corpse sometime between then and when I discovered it Sunday morning.

Why they chose Johnny's place was still a mystery.

I walked to the end of the driveway and ducked under the crime scene tape. The pile of paint-soaked leaves looked like it'd been meticulously dug through, and when I poked around with my toe, I didn't spot any remaining balloon fragments.

The grass between the paint trap and the cabin was trampled flat. I needed to follow that trail and enter the cabin to see if I'd missed anything on my terror-blind visit yesterday. Goose bumps rose on my arms, the chilling effect unsettling in the oppressive heat. What if the body was still in there, the white foot starting to decompose in the humid air?

I chewed the inside of my cheek. That was ridiculous. There was no body in there. The police had removed all evidence, and this was probably just a fool's errand, so I should get it over and done with. I marched to the cabin and walked around the perimeter. Glancing in the first window, I saw that the bed had been stripped clean and the mattress taken away. I followed the shape of the cabin until I reached the front entrance.

The door had been removed and was not in sight. Police tape crisscrossed the gaping hole, and I felt an itch at the back of my brain. It had to do with the door, but it wasn't coming clearly. I stepped forward, peeking around the tape, and imagined I could still smell the metallic tinge of blood. I considered busting through the barrier, and that's when I scratched the itch: Whoever had put the body in Johnny's cabin had broken in, nearly taking the door off its hinges in the process. If Johnny had been involved, he would *not* have needed to break in. Whoever left the body had either been setting him up or had just been looking for a quiet spot to leave the corpse.

Now I could believe Johnny was innocent.

I took a deep breath of fresh lake air.

Chapter 35

I drove to the Fortune Café. I needed to be thoughtful about my next steps, and some iced coffee would do nicely to clear my head. Or at least it would have if I hadn't run into Brando outside. His sleek black hair was tied in a ponytail, and his skin glowed bronze in the July sun. He wore a short-sleeved, button-down shirt, plaid khaki shorts that skimmed his knees, and brown fisherman sandals.

"Hey, little bird! You look hot."

I scowled. Did he mean "hot" as in "good" or "hot" as in "sweaty"? "I *am* hot."

"Yeah, this weather is something else." He glanced upward, as if the sun should explain itself. "Did you hear? The chipmunk statue is being delayed. It won't be here until next week. Bad news."

"Chipmunk?" I squinted. "I thought it was a woodchuck."

"Chipmunk, woodchuck," he said, in a "tomato, tomahto" voice, as he sidled closer. "That means I won't be here to see it installed. Wanna host a going-away party for me?"

I started to pull away, then forced myself to freeze. If I was going to help Johnny, and I had decided I had no choice but to help Johnny as a *friend*, I needed to find out what was up with Brando and Dolly. "What'd you have in mind?"

I tried glancing down submissively at his feet and then back into his eyes because I'd read somewhere that the gesture was appealing to the primal hunter in every man, but I was pretty sure I just looked like I had something in my eye.

"I'm staying at a cabin outside of town," he said, his expression suddenly predatory, "but it's really messy, and I have to be out of there by today, anyways. How about I come over to your place tonight?"

He tried to play with a tendril of my hair, but hesitated when he realized it was sweat soaked. I distracted him with my brightest smile. "That would be great! I'll make us supper. What do you like to eat?"

Brando winked. "*Eating* is one of my favorite parts of parties."

Boy, was this guy transparently grody or what? "Great, I'll grill some tofu and vegetables. You bring a couple bottles of wine."

He raised his eyebrow. "I like a girl who's not afraid to drink. Where do you live?"

I gave him directions, and instead of entering the café, I bopped down to Larry's to pick up some tofu. I made a run past the motel on my way back to my place. Still no Dolly's car.

I cruised home into the wagging tails and warm eyes of my animals. Actually, Tiger Pop only sniffed in my direction, but I could sense a restrained welcome. Luna, like most dogs, was so openhearted that she jumped up on me like I was the last Krispy Kreme outside a Phish concert.

"You guys miss me? Huh? You guys miss me?" I scratched them both behind their ears and didn't let up on Tiger Pop until she purred, against her will. I scooped their food, poured them ice water, filled the bird feeders, and hosed out and refreshed the birdbath. I considered setting the sprinkler in the garden, but it was still ninety-eight degrees, according to my thermometer. The water would evaporate before it'd soak in.

I made a mental note to set the sprinkler out after dark.

Tasks done, I went inside and set my stun gun to charge. Then I sliced and marinated the tofu in Bragg Liquid Aminos and garlic chili paste before slipping it in the fridge. The chilled air from the refrigerator felt heavenly, though it smelled like old cilantro and dill pickles. I dusted, vacuumed, scooped out the litter box, and watered my plants before hopping in a cold shower. In less than two hours, the house and I were clean, but I still hadn't decided what to wear. I wanted to appear attractive to loosen his tongue, but I also didn't want to provide easy access to any erogenous zones. I opted for a pushup bra under a short-sleeved white peasant blouse.

For my bottom half, I debated wearing underwear but couldn't bring myself to do it, no matter how badly I wanted the extra layer. It was too hot, and underwear under shorts or pants had always felt like wearing diapers to me. I settled for cutoff, button-fly Levi's. I slid a delicate silver chain around my left ankle and thin silver hoops in each ear, and dusted sandalwood perfume on my wrists and behind my knees. I twisted my hair into a loose bun at the base of my neck, artfully pulling tendrils down around my face. A little eyeliner, mascara, and lip gloss, and I was as cute as I was gonna get.

Just in time, too. I heard Luna bark as the Hummer pulled up. I couldn't believe I was allowing a man who drove a tank to enter my home. The things a gal was forced to do for her friends. I swallowed my distaste and headed outside to greet him.

He parked the Hummer under the towering lilacs in the middle circle of the driveway and emerged, pausing to stand on his running board like the captain of the *Titanic*. He wore the same button-down shirt and khaki shorts he'd been in earlier, but his hair was loose around his shoulders and so black it appeared blue in the sun.

"Beautiful place you have here," he called out.

"Thank you," I called back. *"Show pony,"* I muttered under my breath.

After he was sure I had a chance to admire him astride his gas-guzzling metal Viagra, he reached in for two bottles of wine and hopped down. "Hope you like pinot grigio."

I liked it better than I liked him. "Is it cold?"

"As ice." He drew out the sibilance of the last word, like a snake.

"Come on in," I said, turning back toward the house. "I'll grab some glasses."

I led the way but was pulled up short by his low wolf whistle. "That is a *beautiful* view."

Something told me he wasn't talking about the lake on the other side of my garden, so I ignored the comment. I held the door for him, so he had to enter the house in front of me. "Want to help me get the grill going?"

"Oooh, no can do. I'm a restaurant kind of man. Don't know anything about grilling. I can open wine, though." He offered me a playful smile.

The effort it took not to roll my eyes almost made me lose my balance. I tossed him a wine opener before I strode out to light the grill. "Glasses are in the cupboard, above the sink." I felt his eyes burn holes into my ass as I walked outside.

"Stop looking at me like that," I hissed at Tiger Pop, as she criticized me from her sunspot on the back deck. "It's not what you think."

She closed her eyes in half-lidded judgment. Luna just watched me eagerly, if a little sadly, as if to say, "Us easy chicks need to stick together, right?" I sighed and turned the grill knobs, tossing a wooden match at it from a safe distance. I'd lost my eyebrows lighting a gas stove as a kid and hadn't gotten within three feet of a combustible situation since. Usually, by the twelfth or thirteenth air-lobbed match, I managed to get the grill going.

Thankfully, tonight was no exception.

"Beautiful night," Brando said as he opened the screen door with his hip, a frosty glass of wine in each hand. "And lovely company."

I reached for the wine, downed half the glass, and smiled up at him. This detecting was doing a number on my sobriety. "How long do you plan to stay in Battle Lake?"

"Don't you remember?" he purred. "Tonight is my going-away party."

I pulled away from his seeking hand. "So you're leaving tomorrow?"

"I have a little business to take care of," he said vaguely. "When it's done, I'll be gone. Shouldn't take more'n a day or two."

"What kind of business?" I tried batting my eyes, but the mascara was gummy, making it look like I was sending an ocular SOS. "You make friends in town?"

He smirked. "I have friends everywhere." Then his eyebrows gathered over his nose. "That grill ready? I'm a hungry man."

I wondered at the change of subject as I strolled past him into the house. I threw back the rest of my wine, refilled my glass, grabbed the marinated tofu and the vegetables I'd skewered, and piled it all on a tray. Except for the mushrooms and red peppers, the vegetables were fresh from my garden—baby potatoes, new onions, miniature zucchini, and cherry tomatoes I'd bought as nearly full-grown plants from Johnny at the greenhouse. I also stacked on the grilling tray meant for fish that I used to keep the tofu from sticking. I balanced the tray on my right hand and opened the door with my left. "Coming through!"

He glanced up, judging me and the food I carried. "You're kind of a granola girl, aren't you, what with all your fresh veggies and your long hair? I love au naturel chicks."

I put down the tray, slammed my second glass of wine as he strolled closer, and held my empty glass like a wall between us. "Can you fill this? You might need to open a new bottle."

He appeared momentarily surprised, his full lips drawing down. "No problem."

While he was in the house, I sprayed down the grill with canola oil and set on the veggies and tofu. The tangy aroma of the marinade dripping onto the flames hit my nose. Brando returned shortly with a refreshed glass of wine for me. "Thank you," I said, accepting it.

"You're welcome. I'm really glad you invited me out here today, Myra."

I coughed. He was seriously going to mispronounce my name while I cooked for him? "It's Mira, like, 'you better stand clear-a.'"

"Mira. Of course." He smiled seductively. "Battle Lake is a quirky little town, you know, and all you people have made me feel so welcome. I might just have to return someday real soon." He set down his wineglass and moved behind me. I willed myself to remain still, like a deer who didn't want to run and expose herself. I didn't even flinch when he started to massage my shoulders.

In fact, it soon began to feel tolerable, even good, cresting on the cozy buzz of a wine high. "You like that, don't you?" he asked, his mouth close to my ear. "You're so tense, and you carry it all in your shoulders. I can feel it melting away now. Can't you?"

I closed my eyes and let my head roll slightly. I really could feel the tension leaving and the wine filling in the cracks. What crap luck that the guy with the Hummer had magic hands. The tofu popped, and so did my eyes. I stepped forward to flip the vegetables and grilling tray, horrified that I'd started to forget what a slimeball this guy was. He'd kissed and told on Kennie, gotten intimate with Dolly, ogled Heaven and Brittany, and was now sniffing around me.

Still, the massage had felt really good. *I could take two steps backward, and I bet he'd start up again where he left off.*

"I *have* been stressed lately," I admitted, reaching to take a deep swallow from my third glass of wine. My head was now swimming nicely.

"I'm sure," he said, his voice coming low and deep from right behind me. "Running the library, writing for the newspaper, keeping the town safe. It's a full-time job." His hand trailed my spine to its base and back up again, his fingers strong and seeking. "You're a real beauty, you know, Mira."

My eyes were half-closed, which was enough to tell that the food was done. I pulled it off the grill, disappointed and relieved that the touching was going to end. I needed to keep my head on straight if I wanted to come out of this interview on top, or at least with my clothes intact. "Do you want to eat inside or out?"

I turned to him, holding the tray of food, and was surprised by the hooded intensity in his gaze. He grabbed the tray out of my hands and set it down on the picnic table near the grill. Before I could object, he pulled my face to his and brushed his mouth against my neck. His lips were strong, and when I instinctively leaned in, they softened and fit to mine. I could feel the taut length of him, and a tremor passed through me. I tried to muster up indignation, outrage, or even disgust at how easy I was, but this guy was *good*. He seemed to have eight hands, in the best possible way.

Maybe he was like olives, I told myself. You had to work hard to like them, but once you did, you couldn't get enough.

For a split second, common sense commandeered the steering wheel and I tried to pull away, but one hand at the small of my back and the other tangled in my hair tugged me again into him, hard. Our kissing was the real deal—no teeth scraping, no awkward tongue wrestling, no unintentional noises. I could taste the sweet flavor of wine on his lips. Research, I'd call this. He'd certainly be much more relaxed with me after we fooled around, and maybe I could get him to spill some secrets then. Johnny had better appreciate what I was doing to set him free.

Johnny.

I jerked my head back and stared into Brando's surprisingly unfamiliar face. What the hell had I been doing? "Um, maybe we should eat."

He cocked his head like a lizard, and his eyes became glacial. An unsettling burst of fear shot through my belly.

"Sure," he said. "Let's eat." He ran his fingers through his hair, never taking his icy eyes off my face.

I picked up the tray of food but was suddenly bone-certain that I better not turn my back on this man. I didn't know what'd triggered his sudden shift from passionate to pissed, but fury was radiating from him like heat waves. Luna had gotten to her feet, her hackles raised, a low growl in her throat.

He seemed not to notice.

"You first," I said, moving aside so he could lead the way inside.

It might have been a standoff if not for the bile-green Gremlin that rumbled down my driveway.

Chapter 36

Both Brando and I watched the car pull up and park behind the Hummer.

"Holy crap! What the hell is that?" Bad Brad snort-laughed as he stepped out of his rusty car and walked admiringly around the Hummer. "Are we at war?"

I watched Brando out of the corner of my eye. Both his anger and his pants deflated slowly but steadily, as if by sheer force of will. By the time Bad Brad reached us, Brando was his suave, good-looking self again. He offered his hand. "That's my ride. Name's Brando."

"Wow! That's a great name. I'm Brad."

I could see the wheels—or more accurately, "wheel"—turning in Brad's head, and I foresaw a name change in the near future for the leader of Not with My Horse. I was too grateful for his presence to make fun of him, though, especially since he no longer wore a lab coat, instead sporting a pair of cutoffs and a tank top that highlighted his farmer's tan.

"Hey, you're just in time," I said to him. "We were about to eat. You hungry?"

"You know I can always eat," he said, smiling. "As long as you guys don't mind. We can celebrate my good news!"

"What's your good news?" I asked, not sure I wanted to hear the answer.

"It looks like I found a job." He clapped his hands, applauding himself. "Everyone's hiring! When I was down at Bonnie & Clyde's, I heard they need construction workers in Fergus Falls. Someone else said I could bartend at Stub's, and some guy even told me there's a nutty professor in town paying good money for workers to tear down statues."

Brando and I glanced at each other. His face was unreadable, and I hoped mine was, too, like a professional gambler holding her cards close to her chest. More likely, however, my right ear looked like a *D*, my right eye looked like an *O*, the furrowed lines between my brows looked like two *L*s, and my left eyebrow looked like a *Y*.

Brando brushed his hand across his mouth and leaned in to kiss my forehead. I winced, whether from the leftover heat between us or fear, I wasn't sure. "Thanks for inviting me out, Mira, but I better head back to town. I need to finish packing."

"Sure," I said. "Maybe some other time."

He gave Brad a curt nod, fired up the tank, and poured out of the driveway with a dramatic rumble.

"What the holy hell is he driving, anyhow? A 1057 All-Desert 10-ton Dune Runner?"

"It's a Hummer, Brad." Now that Brando was gone, I wanted BB gone, too. I'd been through a lot the last few days, and to top it all off, I could feel a thwarted-sex headache forming behind my eyes. "I appreciate you coming when you did, by the way. I'm really tired, though. Can I pack up some food for you to take with?"

Bad Brad looked at me, seriously *looked* at me, for the first time since he'd arrived in Battle Lake. "You do look beat. Why don't you go lay down? I'll clean up and take what I need."

His sudden kindness intensified my guilt for making out with Brando. I took a stab at easing it by clearing up a black mark from my past. "You know how I left Minneapolis without saying goodbye?"

Brad nodded, reaching for a grilled potato.

"It was because I caught you cheating on me. With Ted's niece."

He swallowed and looked at me sheepishly. "I kinda figured. Sorry."

"And I took the nuts off your bike, which is why you crashed it."

Brad started laughing. "No shit? That hurt."

I smiled back at him, relieved by his reaction. "Yeah, well, it was pretty childish, and I'm sorry I did it."

"I deserved it," he said, grabbing for a slab of grill-marked tofu.

"Thanks." I leaned in to give him a hug. It felt good to get that off my chest. I was asleep in my bed before he left.

Chapter 37

When I next opened my eyes, the sky was grim. I sat up so quickly that the room spun for a moment. The digital clock on my nightstand was blinking 12:00 in an acid red, meaning the power had gone out at some point.

A rip of thunder tore across the lake and boom-echoed through the house. My heart caromed off its track and hammered around loose in my chest. Was it Monday night or Tuesday morning? How long had I been asleep? Was I alone in my house?

The smell of ozone, followed by a flash of lightning, unsettled me. I forced myself out of bed and into my kitchen. The battery-powered clock hanging on a nail over the fridge read 8:36, but I didn't know if it was morning or night. What time had I gone to bed? All the stress was taking its toll.

I jumped as Tiger Pop brushed against my leg. "Hey, sweetie." Petting her, I asked, "How long have I been asleep?"

No answer.

I cruised to my front door, which was shut and locked. Brad looking out for me about a year too late. I opened the main door and leaned my face against the cool screen of the outer door. It must be morning, or it would still be warm. I'd slept for more than twelve hours. I watched the first drop of rain hit my garden, scaring up black dust. Then the second drop came, and the third. Just as I remembered I hadn't closed my car windows, the sky opened up.

I dashed to my Toyota, rolled up all four windows, and was drenched right down to the inner seam of my cutoffs by the time I splashed back inside. As the rain pounded down, a wicked-cold breeze slipped like an icy tongue through the wall of heavy air. We were in for a mother of a storm.

"Whaddya think, Tiger Pop? Should I wait it out, or make a dash for town now before it gets even worse?"

"Woof," Luna answered for her.

To town it was.

I considered running out to the car my shower, so I only needed to change clothes and brush my teeth. I got Luna and Tiger Pop fresh food and water and, umbrella in hand, put their vittles in the sheltered area beneath the house. When the rain let up, I knew they'd both want to be outdoors.

The sky was black except for the razors of lightning slicing through. The thunder was the only sound loud enough to trump the hammering rain. Battle Lake was getting itself cleaned behind the ears, sure enough. The farmers were going to be thrilled as long as no hail came with the package.

The drive to town was slow going. At thirty miles per hour, I could just barely make out the hood of my car, and my windshield wipers were doing more stirring than removing. Sid and Nancy, bless their hearts, had opened the Fortune Café, but there wasn't much business. The only other customers were some out-of-towners and their miserable-looking kids ("But honey, we can play Monopoly in here until the rain lets up!"), Les Pastner, and a waitress from the Turtle Stew ordering some real coffee before her shift started.

I stepped in line behind the waitress but was distracted by the sound of radio snaps and burps. Les was seated at the two-top to my immediate left, fiddling with a small radio poorly hidden in his army jacket. To my infinite surprise, he appeared to be drinking a marble mocha macchiato, extra whipped cream, hold the cinnamon. Apparently, even militiamen were not immune to the finer pleasures.

"What're you listening to, Les?"

"Police scanner."

"Any news?"

"Can't hear. The storm is messing up my frequency."

"Mind if I join you after I get my breakfast?"

Les's hair was slicked off to one side with a part you could land a jet on, and his squinty eyes were so deep-set, I couldn't tell what color they were. "Why?"

"You and I need to talk."

He glanced around furtively. The waitress had taken her coffee and left, and Sid and Nancy had politely disappeared into the kitchen. Meanwhile, the family were settled into the back room to see if the Parker Brothers could keep them sane. "You said you weren't gonna tell no one you saw me outside the motel." He sounded accusing.

"And I meant it. I just wanted to ask you if you know if Dolly and Brando came to town together."

Les tried to appear tough, like an impenetrable mafia don, but it wasn't an easy look to pull off with whipped cream on your upper lip. "I'm not working for *you*."

That set me back on my heels. With the emphasis on the "you," Les had tipped his hand a little too far. "But you're working for *someone*." It was a statement, not a question. "Who?"

He took another sip of his gourmet coffee and busied himself fiddling with his radio.

"OK, don't tell me who it is," I said. "What'd they hire you to do?"

A clear stream of words erupted out of the radio, though they sounded distant. Les yanked up the antennae another inch and readjusted them.

"Was it a male or female who hired you, or both?" I persisted.

His radio squawked. ". . . Big Ole statue missing from Alexandria . . ."

My heart skipped, and Les's eyes grew big. He and I were both leaning toward his radio now, our heads almost touching when another clear snatch of conversation came through. "It's just gone. What does someone want with a big Norwegian statue?"

There was a crackle, and then a response from another officer, or the dispatcher. "Ransom? Or maybe Chief Wenonga was getting lonely." Followed by a chuckle. "No scalp on this one?"

"No blood. I repeat, no blood. The statue has just disappeared."

My mouth had gone dry. Another fiberglass statue, this one only forty-five minutes up the road, had been stolen?

I jumped when Les slammed his radio against the tabletop, spilling his coffee. "God bless it! This is not how it was supposed to go!" He ignored the mess he'd made and stormed out of the Fortune Café, radio in hand.

Sid reappeared from the kitchen. "What was that all about?"

I shook my head in amazement. "Les's police scanner. Someone stole Big Ole out of Alexandria."

"No way!" She wiped her hands on the towel she was carrying, and I was shocked to notice she was wearing a skirt. "Well, it looks like our bad luck is spreading around a little. But why's someone stealing schlocky statues?"

I bristled at the "schlocky." The Chief was *sexy*. "Maybe they want to build the world's largest mini golf course?"

Inside, though, my thoughts were spinning. I'd assumed Chief Wenonga was stolen to strike a blow for PEAS, and the missing Randy Myers dressed as a Native American had lent credence to that theory. Now, Randy had turned up, and a non-Native statue had been stolen.

That meant only one thing: this whole thing had *always* been about the statues, not the politics. That pointed the finger squarely at Brando. But how was Dolly involved?

"I don't think it's for mini golf," Sid said. "Where do you hide twenty-plus-foot statues?"

Good question. "I dunno, but I aim to find out. Can I get a sun-dried tomato bagel with provolone cheese, to go? And maybe a Diet Coke. I have a feeling it's going to be a long day."

"Sure thing, shug." She wrapped my food in waxed paper and filled a to-go cup with pop, and I dashed back into the rain. It had let up from "fire hose in the sky" to "water pressure in the average trailer," so I gambled I wouldn't need my umbrella to skedaddle the fifteen feet from the front door to my car.

I lost that bet.

I was soaked for the second time that day. The temperature was seventy-four degrees, according to the bank's LCD screen, so at least it wasn't a miserable soaked.

I drove to the library and shook off inside before firing up the front desk computer. I needed some information, starting with "Big Ole Alexandria Minnesota." The first link pulled up an attractive (if you liked the Nordic type) picture of the statue, horned helmet on his head, blond, shoulder-length locks cascading into his beard and mustache.

He carried a wussy-looking spear in one hand and a shield in the other, with his sword strapped to his waist. He wore a miniskirt that would make Paris Hilton proud. It was bright yellow and skimmed the upper thighs of his unusually long legs. It also highlighted nicely the fact that one leg was raised and stepping forward, as if to say, "I have conquered this land, and I did it in a skirt." It was suggestively sexy, in a homoerotic sort of way. Me, I preferred tall, dark, and handsome. There was something nagging me about that statue, though.

Something *familiar*.

I read the description below the image and was brought up to date on Alexandria history. The town called itself "The Birthplace of America" due to the Kensington Runestone found nearby in 1898. Olof Öhman, an illiterate local farmer, discovered it under the roots of an aspen tree. The markings on the 202-pound stone were believed to be a runic inscription describing a Viking expedition in 1362, a date well preceding Columbus's "discovery" of America. Controversy followed Öhman's finding, with his veracity being called into question.

In 1948, the Smithsonian displayed the runestone, where it stayed for about twenty years until the museum deemed it a fake, returning it to Minnesota. Unfortunately, the Smithsonian curators had used a wire brush to scrub all the micro-evidence that could have dated it. It was apparently quite a scandal, with differing conspiracy theories as to why the museum folks had scoured the stone.

Before the Smithsonian biffed and at the high point of the positive runestone publicity, Alexandria commissioned a twenty-eight-foot fiberglass statue of Ole Oppe, better known as the Viking Big Ole. He began his existence at the World's Fair in 1965 before moving to Alexandria.

I had to search three more sites before I located exactly what I was looking for using the phrase "Ole Oppe Alexandria": the statue had been built by one Fibertastic Enterprises out of Stevens Point, Wisconsin.

Hello, Brando Erikkson. Why, pray tell, are you stealing your own statues? And why scalp Liam Anderson?

I flipped back to my search page and typed in "Fibertastic Enterprises." I'd visited the site earlier but hadn't dug deeply. This time, I was going to uncover something, even if I had to read all 1,314 results.

The first hit was the same home page for the Stevens Point company that I'd come across in my original research. The next hundred or so were links to the websites of communities that'd purchased statues from Fibertastic and were crediting the company. Among those were mentions of Chief Wenonga in Battle Lake and Big Ole in Alexandria. It was at link number 132 that I hit pay dirt in the form of a brief article in the online English version of the *Mumbai Mirror* out of India. The article was titled Gandhi Falls on Jain Passersby, Injuring Many:

> A group of six Jain devotees, on a pilgrimage to Shatrunjaya Hills, were injured as a nearby twenty-five-foot statue of Mahatma Gandhi fell on them. The statue had been commissioned in the late 1970s by a wealthy Brit named Bobcat Perham and intended as a reminder of Gandhi's sacrifices. Fibertastic Enterprises, a Wisconsin, United States, company, built, shipped, and

installed the statue. The statue's fall appeared to be an act of God.

The article included a picture of the Gandhi statue, presumably taken before it toppled over. The statue looked unusually robust, given Gandhi's historically emaciated appearance, and strangely familiar. I contemplated that as I ran the name of the town through my memory. Shatrunjaya Hills.

It took me only a few seconds to remember: when Johnny had called from Wisconsin, he'd said Dolly Castle had studied abroad in Shatrunjaya Hills, India.

The mystery was solved!

Brando, who for all I knew had a hand in creating the Ronald McDonald statues Dolly had vandalized, had built a statue that had injured innocent bystanders. Dolly, swept up in the cause of the unfairly injured Jains, was doling out her own form of weird punishment by stealing his work here in the Midwest. I wondered if her group, PEAS, even existed or if it was just a front for her as she skulked around Battle Lake and Alexandria, publicly humiliating Brando while he was in town to celebrate a Wenonga-less Chief Wenonga Days.

It was time to confront one Dolly Castle, woman to woman.

Chapter 38

Mrs. Berns was only too happy to run the library by herself. "Kennie and I need to meet, anyhow," she said, glancing at the books in the drop-off bin.

That stopped me cold. They normally didn't get along. "What for?"

She shuffled away, not bothering to grab the books. "Never you mind."

I followed her. "Are you two going to start a business?"

"We're just going to hang out and talk."

My Spidey sense was tingling. "But you don't like Kennie."

Mrs. Berns cackled. "I didn't like my husband, either, but that didn't stop me from enjoying his company, if you know what I mean. Now stop worrying and go do whatever gallivanting it is you intend to do."

"OK," I said, uneasy at the thought of the two of them here alone together, "but remember, if anything happens to the library, we're both out of work."

She gave me a curt "Ach!" and sent me on my way.

My first stop was the Battle Lake Motel, where I was grateful to find Dolly's black Honda in the lot. The rain must have kept her inside. I pulled into Halverson Park, not yet sure of my plan. I could either knock on her door and just straight up ask her what was going on or hide in the rain and follow her when she finally left.

I landed on subterfuge and settled in for a wait.

About forty-five minutes passed, and the inside of my windshield grew good and foggy. It was raining too hard to even crack the windows, so I started my car and turned on the defrost. I fiddled with my knob until I tuned in 92.3, the classic rock station out of Alexandria. Led Zeppelin's "When the Levee Breaks" blues-rocked over the airwaves.

I took it as a good omen.

Sure enough, a few minutes later, the doorknob on room number 7 jiggled, and Dolly's head popped out and then back in. When she next emerged, she held an aqua-blue umbrella. She dashed through the downpour into her car, too engrossed in staying dry to notice if she was being watched or followed.

When she pulled out and drove past Halverson Park, I let one car slip between us before following. As far as I knew, she didn't know what my car looked like, but better safe than sorry. She was heading through town, and the traffic was light, likely due to the storm. She stopped at the intersection of 78 and 210, then kept driving south on 78. When she turned east shortly after, I wondered where she was headed. If she was returning to Wisconsin, this wasn't the quickest way to 94. Back here was only a Bible camp, Inspiration Peak, and farms.

My radio lost its signal. I fiddled with static before the entire mechanism began screeching. This happened often in my little Toyota, particularly when it rained. I punched the volume button off and sniffed in the wet green of the Minnesota grassland jungle. To the south of the road was a herd of sodden cows, and to the north were rolling hills dense with sumac and prairie grass. The landscape was covered in sheets of wet gray, the rain falling so fast that it sluiced downhill instead of being absorbed.

I relaxed following Dolly, enjoying the lull of the scenery, and suddenly, as I crested the last hill before Inspiration Peak, she was gone. *Shoot!* The blacktop was empty for the two miles I could see. She must have turned left onto the gravel road that twisted out of sight, the one that led to Inspiration Peak.

I'd visited the peak a few times before, mostly in the fall when the leaves were a blazing quilt of reds, golds, and oranges. At 1,750 feet, approximately 400 feet above the surrounding landscape, it was the highest point in Otter Tail County and the third highest point in all of Minnesota. The rumor was that Sinclair Lewis wrote some of his social criticism there, and that he'd named the summit. It was a thigh-busting straight-up hike to the top but worth every ragged breath. You could see nearly thirty miles in every direction on a clear day.

Was it possible Dolly was just out here for some sightseeing and hiking? Unlikely, given the rain. Still, I might as well check out the dead-end parking lot so I could rule out her having gone that way. I swung a right and wasn't surprised to find the lot was empty. I looped around to head back down the hill when a darker shape in the woods off to my right caught my eye. I rolled down my window and squinted through the rain, making out what appeared to be a hatchback hidden under an enormous sheltering pine.

Dolly's car.

She clearly hadn't wanted to leave it out in the open.

Dangit. I was going to have to get out and see what was up.

In the spirit of staying undercover, I retraced my route to the restaurant at the base of the summit, parked behind the dumpster, grabbed my flashlight, and dragged my miserable butt out into the rain. The downpour had tapered off to a steady shower, and at least it was warm, but it was never fun to be wet in clothes. At least Dolly would be easy to follow in the mud. I backtracked to her car and shined my light in. Empty. Fresh hiking boot tracks, filling up softly with rain under the protection of the hardwoods, led off-trail from her car and into the woods.

I followed.

The oaks and pine kept the worst of the rain away, but the musty smell of wet leaves and pine needles clung to me. It wasn't long before I felt a crawling sensation at the back of my neck—a wood tick, looking for room and board. *Eek!* I pulled it out of my shirt and squished its rubbery body with my thumbnail before flinging it into the woods.

It was all over now.

I had wood tick fever, head to toe, inside and out. Every branch brushing against my skin, every raindrop trickling down my naked arm, every tingle in my scalp was a hungry bloodsucker looking to plunge its fangs into my flesh and grow corpulent, blue-gray and lethargic, like a vampiric blueberry. *Ugh.* I was so caught up in my paranoia that I almost missed the yellow sign warning me that I was leaving state park grounds.

The landscape was changing from hardwoods and some pine to pine and some scrub, to marsh fern and fringed loosestrife—native swamp plants. I was heading into uncertain ground, and it wasn't until my feet made a sucking noise as I pulled them up for a step that I truly glanced around. Dolly's hiking boot trail was still in front of me, though harder to follow now that the trees were no longer protecting it from the rain. And I was definitely entering a swamp. I could tell by the lay of the land and by the boggy, canned-fish smell in the air.

The Inspiration Peak parking lot was now nearly a mile back. In front was what felt like my best chance to free Johnny. I cocked my ear to listen for any sign of Dolly. Nothing but the soft drip-patter of rain and some far-off thunder. I had no choice but to continue, and to add leech fever to my list of worries. Plodding gingerly forward, I put my sandal-shod feet on fallen sticks when possible and sank into the muck when it wasn't. I took solace in the fact that Dolly didn't seem to be having any better time of it than me, judging by her footprints deep in the slime. A half mile later, I was through the swamp and back into the relative comfort of emerald-green prairie grass and shoulder-height red sumac.

Which was where I lost the trail.

I searched frantically, starting at the last footprint and working outward in concentric circles. When I started hitting the swamp again on the far side of the circle, I really began to worry. I hiked up the highest hill, careful to stick close to the ground and make as little noise as possible. From my poor excuse for a perch, I spotted an abandoned farmstead in front of me and Inspiration Peak looming behind. I didn't spot any movement from the farmstead, but it was worth a look-see since I'd come this far.

I made my way carefully toward the sagging barn's rear, its red paint faded to a rusty brown. A tired silo was on one side and, on the other, an abandoned farmhouse, its front windows shattered years ago by teens, or maybe a drunken Sinclair Lewis. A cluster of proud oaks surrounded the old structures, but there were no other buildings. A dirt road, soggy and overgrown with weeds, led away from the farmstead. From this distance, I couldn't tell if it had been used recently.

I was a hundred yards from the barn, sticking close to the ground and behind sumac shrubs, when I spotted movement. Dolly, leaving the house. My skin lifted with satisfaction. I hadn't lost her! The house was doorless, so she simply stepped out of the opening and strode toward the front of the barn. She walked briskly, confidently, not like she was exploring but rather like she was finishing up business, and then she was out of sight.

I studied the short distance between the barn and me. I'd have better luck hiding there than at the edge of the prairie. As if on jungle patrol, I made a quiet dash forward and slapped my back against the barn before dropping to all fours, my bare knees soaking up mud and moisture from the drenched ground. After listening for any nearby movement and hearing none, I crawled to the side of the building and peeked around. Still no human movement, and so I hugged the ground tighter and wormed my way toward the front.

I continued, unmolested, until I heard the soft murmurings of voices. I couldn't make out what they were saying, but it was clearly a man and a woman talking, and they sounded angry. I risked poking my head around and saw that the entire face of the barn was exposed, the sliding door having fallen or been removed from its roller long ago.

I noticed that second. What I noticed first was the two huge, sandal-clad feet sticking out the front of the barn.

Twenty-eight-foot fiberglass-Norse-warrior huge.

Chapter 39

Big Ole!

Did Dolly have Chief Wenonga hidden here, too? I glanced up at the silo, hoping to spy a shock of black hair poking over the top that I'd maybe missed earlier. Before I could get a clear view, Dolly stormed out of the barn, followed by Les. I dived back around the corner, out of sight.

"We agreed on $2,500," Les was saying gruffly. I hadn't gotten a good look at him before I hid, but the rage in his voice was clear.

"I said I'd pay you $2,500 in exchange for two very specific things," Dolly said coolly. "You've only delivered one."

"One *big* one! Not a single person saw me or my brother leave with that statue. That's worth $2,500 alone!"

I bet Dolly was going to say something really important then, something like, "But you messed up getting Chief Wenonga and forced me to murder Liam Anderson, so you're only getting $1,250 and are lucky you're getting anything, and I never even kissed Johnny Leeson because he said he loves Mira James, who's for sure way better in bed than I could ever be," but I'd never know because at that unfortunate moment, a crow squawked behind me. An evil, murderous squawk that would have scared any normal human being out of her skin. When I yelled and jumped away, I landed on the ground near Dolly and Les.

They both stared at me like I'd just plopped out of a cow's behind.

"Hi." That's all I could get out before Les lunged at me, loaded for bear.

He wore munitions strapped across his chest in an X, a knife belt around each skinny thigh, a stun gun at his hip (why hadn't I brought my own blessed stun gun?), and a sword in a scabbard at his back. He landed on top of me and quickly spun my arms and his legs around in circles, twisting my body in some elaborate half-nelson-cross-face-chicken-wing armlock, accompanied by high-pitched Bruce Lee karate sounds.

When he'd forced us both into an ungainly position, confident that I was trapped, he demanded, "How do you like that, missy?"

Unfortunately for him, Les was not a gifted wrestler. He mostly had himself tangled and me by the wrists. A flick of each, and I stood up as he fell harmlessly off me. "It was kind of gross, Les, to be honest." I shuddered. "So, you stole Big Ole?"

Air escaped Dolly in a frustrated *oof.* "Jesus, Les. What was that? I thought you were going to hurt her. You need to be more careful."

I eyeballed Dolly, shocked. "You don't *want* him to hurt me? I could spill the beans about all this." I waved my arm to encompass Big Ole's sandaled feet and generous thighs visible inside the barn. I also glanced quickly up his skirt—*neuter, I knew it*—but I think my peek was suave enough that Dolly didn't notice.

"I don't want *anyone* hurt," she said. "I never did."

"Especially the Jains?" I asked.

Dolly's sea-green eyes narrowed. She was covered in mud up to her knees, her sodden strawberry-blonde hair was escaping her ponytail and plastering itself to her cheeks, and her hands were on her hips so tight I thought they might leave bruises. "You know about the statue in India?"

"I only have theories." No way was I going to tip my hand before she showed me hers. "The one thing I can tell you for sure, though, is that Johnny Leeson is in jail for something he didn't do."

"What?" She appeared genuinely surprised.

"Johnny was arrested yesterday. A dead body was found at his cabin on Silver Lake, some guy from Wisconsin named Liam Anderson." I raised an eyebrow, certain I'd caught her. "Sound familiar?"

"No." Her voice was laced with genuine concern. "The police think Johnny killed him?"

"They do." She really seemed to be telling the truth about not knowing about the body. I'd need to rethink my whole theory. "And this Liam Anderson is missing a chunk of his scalp. Whoever killed him probably also stole the Chief, and it follows that whoever stole the Chief also stole Big Ole."

"See!" Les exploded. "I told you we shouldn't take Ole so close to Wenonga disappearing! You said no one would connect the two, that the police wouldn't be involved. You madwoman. Mad, Indian-lovin' harpy."

Dolly rubbed her temples. "Calm down."

I shook my head, staring from one to the other. "You two took Ole, but not Wenonga?" That would be like breaking into a chocolate store and stealing only the money. "Dolly, you know Les has been following you since you got to town, don't you?"

Dolly's hands left her temples and hung at her sides. She suddenly appeared very, very tired. "Not me. I hired him to follow Brando and get enough information to pin the Chief's disappearance on him." At this point, she glared at Les. "He didn't get me anything."

That was why Les hadn't earned his full $2,500—he'd snatched Big Ole but hadn't dug up any information on Brando. It made sense. The two times I'd seen him skulking around in the shadows, I'd assumed he was following Dolly, but Brando had also been at both locations.

"Why do you think Brando stole Wenonga?" I asked her.

"Not think. *Know.*" She swiped hair off her face and tucked it back into her ponytail. A reluctant smile played at the corners of her generous mouth. "You're quite the snoop, you know that?"

I wrinkled my nose. "I prefer to think of myself as curious. Johnny isn't really involved in this, is he? If you tell me what's going on, I can help to get him out of jail."

She seemed to weigh her options before she began talking. "I was in Shatrunjaya Hills, India, with a study abroad class. While there, I got involved with a group fighting the corporate invasion of the country. McDonald's was the obvious face of the rampant capitalism, and that's where we concentrated our energies. It was small-time civil disobedience at first—cutting off Ronald McDonald's arms, spray-painting anti-big-business messages on the side of the corporate offices, staging protests outside the front doors of the restaurant while dressed as mad cows.

"Then someone in our group blew up a restaurant. No one was hurt, but I realized it'd gone too far. I packed up and was getting ready to leave when I heard about the Gandhi statue. I'd passed it every day on my way to class, and one day, it just fell over. It hurt some people, Jains on their pilgrimage, but it seemed like an accident. That is, until a local investigation revealed that the statue was structurally unsound. It'd only been a matter of time. That's when Brando flew onto the scene, greasing palms and swishing away with the evidence before anyone could press charges. The insurance claims would have put him under."

I wiped a trickle of water from my eyes. "Did you two meet there?"

"No. And it was just coincidence I ended up in Stevens Point, where Fibertastic Enterprises is based. But once that fell in my lap, I knew it was karma. It was up to me to right the wrongs done by Brando Erikkson's company in India. I just didn't know how, at first."

That still didn't make sense. "So, you came up with the plan to humiliate Brando by stealing his statues?"

"*Humiliate* him?" Her chin pulled back. "Wouldn't that be rather childish? No, after researching, I found out that the Gandhi statue, the Big Ole statue, and the Chief Wenonga statue were all created from the same mold. It followed that all three had the same structural deficiencies. If I could verify that, I could prove that the Gandhi statue falling wasn't an accident. Brando would be forced to pay up."

"Huh?" Her car had passed mine about two sentences back. "How could they all three be made from the same mold? Big Ole is at least five feet taller than Chief Wenonga."

"It's all in the legs, sweetie." She stepped aside. "See for yourself."

I entered the barn and let her show me where extra length had been added to Ole's calves and thighs. I'd always thought it was the skirt that made his lower torso appear unnaturally long, but it'd been part of the design. Brando had told me in the coffee shop that oftentimes in his business one mold was reused, with minor design changes to differentiate one statue from another. And that explained the strange familiarity I'd felt when looking at pictures of the Big Ole and Mahatma Gandhi statues.

They were Wenonga's brothers.

"So, why'd you steal Big Ole?" I asked. "Why not just hire an engineer to check him out?"

She grimaced. "That was the original plan. An engineering professor from UW-Stevens Point was supposed to come out this week to examine the Chief Wenonga statue. Then it was stolen. I had a hunch it was Brando, and if I let him get Big Ole, too, there goes any chance of me connecting him to the India crime. So I rearranged my plans and paid Mr. Militia here to borrow Big Ole for me until the engineering prof could come and check him out. He's supposed to meet me here today."

I felt dizzy and put my hand on Big Ole's thigh to settle myself. So much information to digest. I returned to the beginning. "You said you think Brando stole Chief Wenonga."

"I *know* he did," she said. "Who else could it be? I just don't know how to prove it. My best guess is that Liam Anderson was helping him, but that he has no traceable connections to Brando and was the only witness, which is why he was killed. Brando is evil, and he's devious."

I agreed. I was falling for her story, lock, stock, and smoking barrel, when a realization slapped me across the face like a soap opera star. "But you *slept* with him. I saw him leaving your motel room the night before last. Les saw it, too."

Les nodded smugly.

Dolly's cheeks reddened, and she shrugged. "I figured it'd be easier to sleep with him and find out what he knew than steal Big Ole out of Alexandria. I ended up having to do both."

There, but for the grace of God. I could hardly judge the woman, given the loin-rubbing I'd done with the weasel last night. Speaking of . . . I couldn't help myself. "Was he good?"

She nodded ruefully, her eyes bright with memory. "I'm sorry to say he was fantastic. A truly delicious lover."

Son of a gun.

"But watch out. He seems shallow and pretty, but he's dangerous. Vindictive, narcissistic, and smart as a snake. Good luck connecting him to any of this. I don't know how you're going to get Johnny out of jail."

Which begged another question for me. "Dolly?"

She was massaging the bridge of her nose. "Yeah?"

It was now or never. "Did you sleep with Johnny, too?"

She snorted. "I wish. No, all he wanted to do was talk about Stevens Point and my teaching. At first I was flattered, but then it got kind of boring."

"So why'd you go to his cabin?"

"How'd you know about that?" She eyed Les suspiciously, maybe wondering if he was working both sides.

"I saw you leaving," I lied.

"Saturday night, after the fireworks? Yeah, I thought I would give it one last shot. Figured I'd try the old 'sneak into his bed' trick. When I got there, though, the door looked broken in and Johnny's car was gone. I left."

The old "sneak into his bed" trick? I could scarcely talk to a man I had a crush on, let alone crawl into his bed uninvited. You'd think a quality like that would have bred itself out over a generation or two, but here I was. "Saturday night was the *only* night you were there?"

"Yep. Haven't seen Johnny since."

That squared. Johnny said he'd left town after the fireworks. "So what's next?"

She dropped her hand and looked me in the eye. "I intend to go to the police as soon as my colleague comes to examine Big Ole. I'll nail Brando for India, that I'm sure of. As far as connecting him to Wenonga and the dead Liam Anderson, I'm afraid that will only ever be speculation, unless you receive some divine inspiration. Brando is thorough, and he doesn't leave a trail."

Ice settled in my stomach. That wasn't good enough. I needed to spring Johnny, the sooner the better, and I needed Brando to be held accountable for his crimes, all of them. "When's your engineering professor coming?"

"Within the hour. He's got a Jeep, so he should be able to drive instead of walk. You're welcome to stay and see what he finds."

"No, I need to find a way to tie all of this—not just the statue in India—to Brando." I nodded, displaying far more courage than I felt. "Let me know when he gets busted for the Gandhi statue, though, won't you? I'd love to be there."

Dolly winked. "It's a date. But Mira, don't underestimate him. Please."

Her seriousness chilled me. I trudged back the way I came, smarter but no happier. Even the rainbow that I glimpsed through the tops of the glistening pine trees did nothing to lift my spirits. When I finally made it back to my car, I was hot, wet, and pocked with mosquito bites. I motored to Battle Lake, so lost in my internal dark cloud that I didn't notice I was on a strange gravel road. I decided to keep going forward—all gravel in Minnesota leads to blacktop eventually—and that's how I happened upon the enormous Virgin Mary on the side of the road.

It was another statue, twenty or so feet tall, and it had a sign in front that read Our Lady of the Hills. I parked my car at the side of the road and got out, half-perturbed (*how many frickin' gigantic statues did one county need?*) and half-enraptured. The statue was beautiful. Her face was peaceful, and her straight brown hair and long blue robes blended nicely with the green pines she was tucked among. I walked closer and reached a locked box for offerings. I dropped in a dollar bill and continued to her feet.

The statue seemed to be gazing out at a far-off place where there were answers. I pulled myself up onto her base, careful not to disturb her space, and stood on my tippy-toes to peek inside her cupped hands. They were full of rainwater, only it was reddish from decomposing leaves trapped in the pools of her hands.

And that's when I knew how I'd nail Brando.

Divine inspiration, indeed.

Chapter 40

I sped into town with one goal: I had to find Brando's vehicle, the embarrassingly oversize red Hummer. He'd told me he was leaving town today, but I had a hunch that the missing Big Ole situation was going to delay his exit. Our Lady of the Hills had shown me how to connect Brando to Liam Anderson's corpse, but he needed to be in town for me to pull it off.

My Toyota was pushing seventy as I crested the divided-road hill heading into Battle Lake. I was too antsy to fiddle with my radio, so I tried to relax by concentrating on the weather. The thick, soggy storm clouds were finally clearing, and the air smelled green, clean, and sauna hot. The road moisture was starting to evaporate, leaving sluggish worms to fend for themselves. I tried to avoid as many as I could, but the highway was flush with them.

I knew my first stop should be the cabin Brando had stayed at north of town to see if he had extended his stay. I didn't know exactly *where* north of town, but all it took was a quick stop at the Fortune Café, where Sid said she'd heard he was staying at Nifty Nook Resort on Otter Tail Lake. I buzzed out there and had his cabin pointed out to me by the friendly owners, who I knew from their regular visits to the library. They said he was booked for a few more days, but they didn't think he was around at the moment.

I walked over to the cabin to be sure. Brando's Hummer wasn't in sight and a quick peek in the windows revealed an immaculate if small interior. The kitchen was spotless, with daisy-strewn curtains cutting the sunlight. The main room held a couch, a television, a game table, and a bookshelf, and the bedroom had a bed so tightly made, the spread looked like a tourniquet. My guess was that Brando had been so successful at bed-hopping in Battle Lake that he'd rarely, if ever, used this cabin.

I listened to the water of Otter Tail Lake lapping onto the sandy beach and considered my next move. Probably, I'd return to town and ask around to see if anyone had seen Brando. If nothing else, Gina always had her ear to the ground. I decided a quick cruise through the back streets would be a good place to start before hunting her down. There were really only seven avenues off Lake Street anyhow.

It was at the third street, in front of Kennie's house, that I stumbled across the parked Hummer. That woman certainly was taking her job as mayor and one-woman welcome committee seriously.

I parked, scarcely able to contain my excitement, and ran over to the vehicle. It didn't take long—gingerly crouched down on my hands and knees—to find exactly what I was looking for: red paint splashed onto all four wheel wells. The Virgin Mary's leaf stigmata had made me think of it. I hadn't noticed the paint yesterday because of the Hummer's near-matching color.

It *was* Brando who'd originally broken the balloons when he dropped off the dead or dying Liam Anderson into what he must have assumed were empty cabins. Dolly had come by later, unknowingly picked up some of the paint, and turned around when she saw Johnny wasn't there and his door was awry.

Dolly was surely correct that Brando had hired Liam Anderson to help him remove the statue. Anderson must have slipped or had something dropped on him in the process. Brando, apparently not one to be troubled by his heart or conscience, hadn't brought his partner to the hospital. He must have been scouting out a hiding place to unload his hireling when he stumbled across Johnny's cabin.

It wasn't teenagers spinning shitties there on Friday; it was Brando looking for a place to stash the dying man. I shuddered at the horrific coldness of it.

What Brando hadn't planned for was the paint-filled balloons Johnny had secreted under the pile of leaves. I'd been too fixated on Dolly as the criminal to even check Brando's car before today. Now I had hard evidence to bring to Gary Wohnt. With the help of Dolly's testimony about when she'd visited Johnny's and what she'd seen there, I could prove that Brando had visited the cabin Saturday night. That would at least be enough to launch an investigation.

It had to be.

"See anything you like?"

I stood so fast that I scraped my head on the wheel well. I whirled on Brando. His features were the same shape as before, but there was an ugly cast to them. All his flirting and salesmanship were gone, leaving a very disturbed, very angry-looking man.

"Not so much," I said, wiping my hands and knees. My heart was thudding. Why were the streets empty? "Paying a house call to Kennie?"

"Something like that." His eyes were two black pins holding my wings in place. He pointed at the rear of his car without breaking that terrifying gaze. "What were you doing down there?"

I rubbed the tender spot on my noggin and pulled my hand away. Blood. This man had a gift for separating people from chunks of their head. "I dropped a bracelet."

Brando stepped toward me, suddenly oozing sexuality and charm. The mood switch was bewildering. "I've never seen you wear a bracelet," he said. He circled my wrist with his large hand and caressed it. "You've got beautiful hands."

"Thank you. I—" Before I could make my goodbyes, Brando clamped down on my arm and twisted it around and back, forcing me to turn with him to keep it from snapping. The pain sent hot mercury streaks up my arm. The world went black and thudding as adrenaline rocketed through my veins.

"I think we need to go for a drive," he hissed in my ear. "You'll like riding in the Hummer. You'll feel on top of the world."

He pushed me toward the vehicle. His left hand opened the driver's-side door as his right held me effortlessly. He gave my arm an extra twist, and I felt more than heard a pop. My knees buckled as he shoved me up and forward. My arm felt attached to my body by only one stretched sinew, and to do anything but lurch forward would have snapped it free. How was this happening in broad daylight?

I had one leg in the car when I spotted the rust-colored stains peeking out from under a towel spread on the seat and carpeting. My mouth filled with saliva. He caught my gaze. "Time to get this reupholstered, don't you think? That's for tomorrow. I have a good friend who owes me a favor. For today, I think we'll just take a little joyride."

Tears started spilling down my face despite myself. His grip was too tight to allow me to turn and look up and down the street, but I knew no one had been outside when I pulled up, and it was too much to hope that Kennie would come out and save me. I couldn't fight without more damage to my arm. I was going to be like Liam, just a dead body with cold white feet, dumped in an empty cabin somewhere. I moaned.

"Shut it." Brando pushed me all the way across the driver's seat and gave a high-pitched screech, which I mistook for sick glee. But then the pressure eased off my arm as quickly as it had come. The lack of pain was exquisite. My arm hung limply at my side, not broken but not right, either. I turned to kick at him but was stopped short by a sight.

Brando was on his knees in an awkward genuflection, his face resting on the pavement. Mrs. Berns stood behind him, crouched down, with one hand between his legs like a cocky quarterback taking the ball from her center. She aimed a rakish grin at me. "I took a class on women's self-defense. What you do, you make a little crook, like so, with your thumb and forefinger and come up from behind and through the legs."

She demonstrated with her free hand. "You squeeze that crook around the very top of the sack like you're castrating a pig, pinch, and twist until something gives." She gave her hand a wicked spin. "That way, you really get their attention."

Or at least you would if they didn't black out from the pain first.

Chapter 41

It took three days and a couple search warrants to find out I'd been mostly right about Brando and Liam Anderson. Brando had hired Liam as muscle to help him remove the statue. According to Brando, Liam had slipped and fallen in the process. He'd scraped his head on the post on the way down. In Minnesota, there was no law requiring someone to bring another person to the hospital, no matter how dire their straits, so the death of Liam Anderson was ruled an accident, and no charges were filed.

However, Dolly's engineering friend found a structural flaw in Big Ole that would have eventually resulted in him crushing some poor sap just trying to get a peek up that skirt. The engineer estimated the structure would have given way in the next year if it hadn't been fixed. Which it was.

It required trimming thirteen inches of thigh off the big guy, but he looked better for it. Now he was as safe as Sesame Street. The discovery of Ole's anatomical flaw had been enough to grant a search warrant for Fibertastic Enterprises, where the dismantled Gandhi was found stowed away in a back storeroom. Apparently, Brando had intended to resell the upper torso to a mini golf course in Branson, Missouri.

There was enough statue left to prove that the same structural flaw that had threatened Big Ole had also sent the Gandhi statue tumbling. It looked like Brando was going to have to pay big to the Jains. His name and photo were on the cover of every newspaper in the Midwest, so he was humiliated as well as financially ruined. Add on to that criminal charges for stealing the Chief, breaking into Johnny's cabin, and assaulting me, and Brando was good and done.

That wasn't even the best news, though: they found my man!

Brando had parked his Hummer with the dead or dying Liam in it in the woods near Johnny's and driven the tractor trailer containing Chief Wenonga all the way back to Stevens Point. There, it had been unloaded, and Brando had left instructions to have Wenonga's body spray-painted white, his hair spray-painted blond, his eyes blue, his leather pants replaced with a half robe, and the tomahawk replaced with a cross.

You guessed it—my emotionally distant hunka hunka burning love had been *this* close to being reincarnated as a fiberglass Jesus. Fortunately, the workers hadn't begun yet.

Thank god for miracles.

Speaking of, it was at the Return of the Chief party held at Halverson Park that Mrs. Berns explained how she inexplicably came to be outside Kennie's house just in time to save me.

"Oh, that? Well, the library was kinda slow, and Kennie and I had that meeting scheduled, but she didn't want to leave because of the rain. So I locked 'er up and headed over. As you guessed, we're starting a new business together."

I wiggled the fingers sticking out of my sling. The doctor said I'd pulled ligaments and gave me a sling and prescribed some truly worthwhile painkillers. They were even better than NyQuil. I wasn't so medicated that I lost all sense, however. I debated whether Mrs. Berns's work ethic and her business venture with Kennie were topics worth pursuing.

I decided to keep it vague. "Yeah?"

"Yeah," she said. "I think Kennie's really got something this time, too. It's an online business."

My shoulders relaxed marginally. "Oh, that's great! Online businesses are really taking off. You have a wider market that way."

Mrs. Berns nodded as if she already knew that. "It's going to be called 'Come Again.' We'll sell previously owned, gently used marital aids. Kennie says it's an untapped market, what with the cost of some of those things new. And you break up with someone or get divorced, you don't want their zingers and buzzers lying around."

Technically, all true. I stared across the crowd. "It sure is a beautiful day to get Wenonga back."

Brando's brother, Peter Erikkson, was now in charge of what was left of Fibertastic and had promised to work around the clock to deliver a retouched Chief Wenonga back to Battle Lake.

He was true to his word, and today was the grand unveiling.

Kennie had arranged for the high school marching band to be present. They'd originally wanted to play "Apache," but Dolly, who'd accepted the new, unpaid position as Battle Lake's honorary historical consultant as well as head of the new diversity advisory panel, had suggested they play something less culturally weighted.

Hence "Eye of the Tiger."

In the first meeting of the diversity advisory panel, held immediately after the Chief statue was discovered in Wisconsin, it'd been decided that Chief Wenonga and Chief Wenonga Days were here to stay, but the festivities going forward would be a true celebration of the First Nation people as well as the immigrants who had since arrived. That might still include turtle races, a street dance, and an all-town garage sale, but it would also include historical tours through Glendalough, no more stereotypical representations of Native Americans in the parade, and introspective pieces in the *Recall*. There was even talk of changing the name of Wenonga Days to the Heritage Festival.

Change could be good, I thought, shading my eyes against the late-afternoon sun that reflected gloriously off the Chief's ebony hair. There were at least two hundred people in Halverson Park doing the same, many of them tourists. Business was booming, thanks to the nation-wide publicity around Wenonga's and Ole's disappearances. I searched for Sid or Nancy, knowing one of them would be here. I felt a tap on my shoulder.

"Mira?"

I turned. It was Johnny, still tanned, rippling, and smelling of vanilla and warm earth despite his brief time in the clink. Other than the tired pull around his eyes and his hesitant smile, he seemed to be all right.

I returned his smile. I was feeling sore and exhausted myself, but confident in a way I hadn't before. I may have gotten my ass handed to me by Brando, but I'd also been part of bringing him to justice. So it was with this new sense of self that I addressed Johnny. "You look so hot."

His mouth quirked. "What?"

I mentally face-palmed myself. My sense of self had lasted all of two seconds. "You look *shot*. That's what I said. It's something we used to say in Paynesville. You know, like 'you look kind of tired.' Guess that saying didn't make it over to Wisconsin." I giggled a tad hysterically and fought the urge to pull out my painkillers and convince him I had a prescription to be stupid.

"No, I guess it didn't," he said. He rubbed his hands across the front of his jeans, glanced in my eyes, and looked hastily away. "I heard you helped bring the Chief back."

"No, that was all Dolly." Credit where credit was due. "You were right to check her out, you know. She had all the information."

He lifted a corner of his mouth. "I thought she stole the Chief."

I nodded. "Yeah, me too."

"Mira?" This time he held my gaze. His eyes were a deeper blue than I'd ever seen them. I had to struggle not to look away from their intensity. "I heard *you* helped me get out of jail."

"Oh, that would have happened sooner or later."

He reached for my arm, glanced angrily at my sling, and pulled back. "You believed in me, and that matters."

It was too much, this vulnerability, this concern. I was going to cry or hump his leg, neither of which I wanted accompanied by "Eye of the Tiger" and an audience. I twisted to lose myself in the crowd, but not before he reached for my uninjured hand.

"Wait," he said.

I turned back, and our gazes held for a beat. I thought I saw a kiss in his eyes before they dropped. It gave me the good shivers.

"I owe you an apology," he said. "I'm sorry I lied about what I was up to in Wisconsin. I should have given you all the information so you could make up your own mind. I also want to thank you for believing in me when I'd given you no reason to. I want to be worthy of that trust."

I nodded, wondering why my fight-or-flight mechanism was kicking in. Johnny wanted to thank me, and if I let it happen, it could be the best thank-you ever. That's when his cell phone buzzed against his hip.

He reluctantly reached for it and got a worried look when he saw the number. "It's my mom. I have to take it."

He stepped away, leaving me vibrating. Was this my chance to fall for a good guy? I couldn't hold a thought, but when he turned back, the concerned look was on his face for a different reason. "I'm sorry, I have to go. My mom hasn't seen me since I got out of jail, and I need to show her I'm all right."

My disappointment was palpable, but how upset could you be with a guy who worried about his mom? "Of course. I appreciate the apology. And the thank-you."

He pushed a stray hair off my cheek, and I think I saw sparks *and* smelled smoke. "I have another thank-you, a better one, I hope. I can come over tonight," he said, his voice husky. "Will you be around?"

Do Norwegians like white food? "I think so."

"I'll knock three times." He smiled his shy grin and walked away.

Chapter 42

I hurried home to get shaved as best I could with one arm, brushed, and perfumed—no beer and eggs in my hair this time—and was ready like a rocket. If I was going to do this, I was going to do it 100 percent.

It went without saying that this was my last shot at a healthy relationship, of course. If it didn't work with Johnny, it was either the nunnery or a quick trip back to the Cities to finish my grad program and become a cat-collecting, asexual English professor (truly, not the worst fate).

I'd reread Dr. Bundy's note when I got home from the Return of the Chief party:

> Dear Mira:
> You are missed! I need a research assistant this fall, and you're my woman. Pay is meager, but your tuition would be free. Is it a deal? Respond at your convenience, as long as it's before August.
> Sincerely yours,
> Dr. Michael Bundy

Smoothing the note on my countertop, I made a deal with myself. If Johnny showed up, I'd give him a chance. I'd open up to him in every way I could. If he didn't show, or if he came and turned out to be like every other guy I'd ever been with except for Jeff, I was packing it up and moving back to the Cities. No one could say I hadn't given Battle Lake a chance.

But, *oh*, did I hope that Johnny would do right by me tonight.

I tried to read and watch TV but spent most of the time squirming and beaming at my animals. *Johnny Leeson is coming over!* I watched anxiously for the telltale headlights down the driveway, the clock ticking a happy beat.

The beat, however, soon grew monotonous, and then taunting. At first, I consoled myself by pointing out that Johnny had just said "tonight," and not given a specific time. Then I moved on to worrying. Johnny was a decent guy, and he would've called to cancel if he could have. By 11:00 p.m., however, I decided that Johnny had had second thoughts.

Fine.

It probably would have had a terrible ending anyhow, with me finding out he was a lousy lover, or collected toenail clippings, or was emotionally distant and unable to commit to a relationship even though we both really liked each other and had buckets in common.

That's what I was telling myself as I walked past my front door, angrily ripping off the cute T-shirt I'd chosen just for the occasion, the one that actually made me look like I had boobs. When, I wondered fiercely, would relationships with men stop being painful experiences I had to learn from and instead be nurturing ones I could grow in?

Never. Absolutely never.

I rubbed hot tears from my eyes, mad at myself for even getting my hopes up. It was the cloister for me, or maybe a job teaching English at a rural technical college.

That's when the first knock came. My breath caught, and I quickly pulled my T-shirt back on. I hadn't heard or seen a car. When the second knock sounded, my heart and loins did a little leprechaun kick. What was on the other side of that door was going to decide whether I returned to the U of M to be Dr. Michael Bundy's research assistant or stayed in Battle Lake a little longer.

Instead of waiting for the third knock, I ripped open the door, naked hope in my eyes. The hope quickly turned to shock, and then confusion.

Actually, I shouldn't have been surprised.

This was Battle Lake, after all. Anything could happen here, and it usually did.

Acknowledgments

First, I'd like to thank my poor TV reception. If not for a pitiable selection of channels, I would write much less. Second, I'd like to extend a heartfelt thanks to my lackluster social life. Because of those endless nights at home, *Knee High* was able to see the light of day. Third, and most importantly, thank you to my mom for coming to watch the kids so I could write, and big love to my children, who inspire me to evolve and grab all that life has to offer.

I've also been remiss in my earlier novels in not thanking the people of Battle Lake, who are good sports about the fun-poking and murder-creating I do in their beautiful town. If you've never been to Battle Lake, go. It's worth the drive.

Finally, thank you to you, dear reader. This would be a lot less fun for me without you.

P.S. Chief Wenonga is just as sexy-hot as you think he is. Also, he has his own Facebook page now??? I swear I had nothing to do with this.

Book Club Questions

1. Red herrings in mysteries are clues that lead the reader astray. Which red herrings did you notice in *Knee High by the Fourth of July*, and which were most effective?

2. Battle Lake is a real town in Minnesota. In what ways can you relate to this setting, and how does it move the story forward?

3. How central is the setting to the book's plot and character?

4. In what way does Dr. Dolly Castle serve as a "foil" for Mira? In what way is she a "double"?

5. Mira James is independent, not afraid of her sexuality, and willing to speak her mind. How would the series be different if she were in a relationship, or shy, or less colorful in her language? Would a relationship with Johnny Leeson change the tone of the book?

6. Similarly, Mira is plagued by her past, as many of us are. How do her previous trials, traumas, and tragedies influence her actions in her current adventures?

7. Consider other contemporary female protagonists in mystery: Stephanie Plum, Kinsey Millhone, Tess Monaghan, and so on. What makes for a lasting female protagonist?

8. On a related note, how does Mira James compare with other female sleuths? What makes her different?

9. The Murder by Month mysteries have been categorized

as everything from amateur sleuth tales (mysteries with a reluctant yet plucky "everywoman" at the center of the action) to cozies (lighter mysteries with no graphic sex or violence and often a small-town setting) to humorous or comic caper mysteries (mysteries where laughs go hand in hand with crime solving). Which of these three categories would you put *Knee High by the Fourth of July* into, and why?

10. Although the central mystery of *Knee High by the Fourth of July* is wrapped up at the end of the book, another mystery begins. Who would you like to see at Mira's door?

About the Author

Photo © 2023 Kelly Weaver Photography

Jess Lourey writes about secrets. She's the bestselling author of thrillers, comic caper mysteries, book club fiction, young adult fiction, and non-fiction. Winner of the Anthony, Thriller, and Minnesota Book Awards, Jess is also an Edgar, Agatha, and Lefty Award–nominated author; TEDx presenter; and recipient of The Loft's Excellence in Teaching fellowship. Check out her TEDx Talk for the true story behind her debut novel, *May Day*. She lives in Minneapolis with a rotating batch of foster kittens (and occasional foster puppies, but those goobers are a lot of work). For more information, visit www.jessicalourey.com.